Kristy and the Worst Kid Ever

**Other books by
Ann M. Martin**

Ma and Pa Dracula
Yours Turly, Shirley
Ten Kids, No Pets
Slam Book
Just a Summer Romance
Missing Since Monday
With You and Without You
Me and Katie (the Pest)
Stage Fright
Inside Out
Bummer Summer

BABY-SITTERS LITTLE SISTER series
THE BABY-SITTERS CLUB series
THE BABY-SITTERS CLUB mysteries
(see back of the book for a more complete listing)

Kristy and the Worst Kid Ever
Ann M. Martin

AN
APPLE
PAPERBACK

SCHOLASTIC INC.
New York Toronto London Auckland Sydney

The author gratefully acknowledges
Nola Thacker
for her help in
preparing this manuscript.

Cover art by Hodges Soileau

ISBN 0-590-45664-4

12 11 10 9 8 7 6 5 4 3 2 1   3 4 5 6 7 8/9

Printed in the U.S.A.   40

First Scholastic printing, March 1993

CHAPTER 1

You remember in *The Wizard of Oz* when Dorothy clicks her heels together three times and says "There's no place like home"? I was thinking about that on one of those cool days which was perfect for running around and playing shrieking-shouting-laughing-jumping games, which is what my brother David Michael and my stepbrother Andrew, my stepsister Karen and my adopted sister Emily Michelle were doing, along with Shannon, our Bernese mountain dog puppy. I was sitting under a tree, watching the kids.

Perfect weather aside, it was a typical Saturday on a typical weekend for my family. My mother was running errands while my stepfather Watson, and Nannie, my grandmother, had left in Nannie's car (the Pink Clinker — it's painted pink) to go scope out a sale at the local gardening center. My brother Sam, who is fifteen, was at his part-time job delivering groceries for the A&P. And my other brother, Charlie, had taken his car, the Junk Bucket (you can guess why it's named that!) to the garage for a tune-up.

As I watched the kids, Karen held the ball up above her head and said to Shannon, "Okay, Shannon, can you say *ball*?"

Shannon promptly sat down, her furry tail sweeping arcs in the leaves on the ground.

"*Ball*, Shannon," Karen coaxed her.

I wasn't too surprised that Karen was urging a dog to talk. She has a very vivid imagination.

"*Ball*," said Karen again.

Shannon barked.

"Good dog," cried Karen, which made Shannon jump up and bark some more.

"Okay, okay," Karen told Shannon. "We'll keep playing."

As Karen threw the ball to David Michael and the game of keep-the-ball-away-from-Shannon started again, I had to laugh at my own thoughts. It might be a typical weekend for me and my family, but I bet it would sound pretty wild to some people. There truly was no place like home — our home, especially!

And since it isn't exactly typical, I guess I'd better explain a little more about it.

I'm Kristy Thomas. I live in Stoneybrook, Connecticut, where I go to Stoneybrook Middle School, coach a softball team called the

Krushers, and am president of the Baby-sitters Club (more about that later). My father walked out on my family when I was just a little kid and lives in California now. We don't hear from him much anymore.

But then my mom got married again, to my stepfather, Watson Brewer. Watson is rich, really rich, and we live in a huge house — a mansion, in fact. That sounds weird all by itself, at least to me, but it's not too bad. I admit I didn't want to move at first. But I also have to admit that having all the extra space is nice. In our old house, for example, my brothers Sam and Charlie had to share a room while David Michael's room was the size of a closet.

But a mansion like Watson's is big enough for everyone to have his or her own room — even though we are filling up the rooms pretty fast, as you can see. Watson's two kids, Karen, who is seven, and Andrew, who is almost five, spend every other weekend with us, plus some holidays and two weeks in the summer. Then there's Emily Michelle, who's our adopted sister. (She's two and a half and is from Vietnam.) Plus there's Nannie, who's Mom's mom. Watson and Mom asked her to come live with us to help out with Emily while the rest of us are at work or at school. So Nannie did.

Of course, Shannon doesn't have her own room (although she does spend a lot of time in David Michael's room!), but she's part of the family. Shannon came to live with us after our collie Louie died. Louie was David Michael's special dog, and we all still miss him. But Shannon's pretty special, too.

And I better not forget Boo-Boo, Watson's big old gray cat with yellow eyes (who has very definite opinions and doesn't mind letting you know them) or the goldfish, Crystal Light the Second and Goldfishie, who belong to Karen and Andrew.

"Okay," Karen announced. "We're going to play 'Where's the ball?' David Michael, you cover Shannon's eyes with your hands and then we'll hide the ball and see if she can find it."

David Michael covered Shannon's eyes (which is not easy with a big, squirming ball of fur like Shannon) while Emily Michelle and Andrew watched. Emily looked on with that sort of benign attention of two-and-a-half year olds, Andrew more seriously. Andrew's not crazy about dogs, although he liked Louie and he likes Shannon, too.

Karen ran over to the picnic table and put the ball in the notch of the table legs, then ran back to David Michael and Shannon.

"Now," she said.

David Michael let go of Shannon, who bounced up expectantly.

Karen held out her hands. "Where's your ball, Shannon?" she asked.

Shannon cocked her head, then looked at everyone else.

David Michael and Andrew held out their empty hands to show they didn't have the ball either.

"Where's your ball, Shannon?" David Michael repeated. "Find your ball."

"Ball!" said Emily Michelle and then threw up her hands. She teetered for a minute, then, with a surprised look on her face, sat down hard.

I jumped up, but before I could run to her, Shannon licked Emily Michelle's face and sat down with her.

"Ball!" said Emily Michelle again, and everyone started laughing, including Emily.

Then David Michael helped her up and Karen said, "We need to give Shannon a *hint*. Shannon, *table*."

I almost started laughing again at the serious expression on Karen's face, and the goofy one on Shannon's as she cocked her head at what Karen said. But I was distracted when I heard voices nearby.

A moment later, I saw Linny and Hannie Papadakis, who live across the street from us and one house down. Linny, who is nine, is David Michael's good friend. Hannie (that's short for Hannah) is seven and goes to school at Stoneybrook Academy where she and Karen are in the same class. Hannie is one of Karen's best friends, along with Nancy Dawes, who lives next door to Karen at her mother's house. Karen, Hannie, and Nancy call themselves the Three Musketeers.

"Hi!" I called.

"Hannie, hi!" called Karen, swooping out of the game and running to her friend.

"Guess what," Hannie said breathlessly.

"You won a trip to the moon!" replied Karen instantly.

I tried hard to keep a straight face. It was just like Karen to answer Hannie that way. I mean, most of the time, when people say, "Guess what?" you're expected to reply, "What?" But not Karen.

"No," said Hannie. "We — "

"Someone left a basket of nine kittens on your doorstep and you get to *keep them all*," said Karen.

"No!" cried Hannie impatiently.

By this time, everyone else had joined Hannie and Karen, even Emily Michelle, who was holding on to David Michael's pants leg.

"You — " Karen began again.

Seeing Hannie's look of annoyance, I said

gently, "Wait a minute, Karen. I think Hannie and Linny have some news for us."

"We're going to become a foster family!" Linny burst out.

"Wow," said Karen. Then she frowned.

"What's a foster family?" said Andrew.

"Is it a family made of adopted people?" guessed David Michael.

"Not exactly," I said. "Foster families are families that sort of temporarily adopt children."

"*Not* like Emily Michelle," said Karen, still frowning. "She's ours always."

Hearing her name, Emily smiled.

"That's right. This is a different kind of arrangement, a special one, like staying with relatives for awhile."

Karen's frown cleared. "Like being a Two-Two?" That's what Karen calls Andrew and herself, because they have two houses and two families and two of almost everything.

"A little like that," I said. "A foster family is a family a kid can stay with when his own parents can't take care of him. After he stays with his foster family for awhile, he can go back to his own family, or to relatives, or even to a brand new family, like Emily Michelle did — one that *is* going to adopt him."

"Neat. Do you get to pick who stays at your house, Hannie?" asked Karen. "Pick a girl.

Then we can be the Four Musketeers, maybe."

"I think you should pick a boy," said David Michael instantly.

"I don't think we get to pick," said Linny.

"Well, I hope your new foster brother is a boy, anyway," said David Michael. "So does Andrew. Don't you, Andrew?"

Andrew nodded.

Hannie shook her head. "Well, we want a foster *sister*."

"Right," agreed Karen.

Just then Shannon came crashing into the middle of us.

"She found her ball!" said David Michael. "*Good* girl. *Good* girl, Shannon. Come on, Linny. Shannon knows a new trick. I'll show it to you."

"Can you stay?" Karen asked Hannie.

"For a little while," said Hannie. "Let's call Nancy and see if she can come over. Is that all right, Kristy?"

"Sure," I said. While the girls were in the house making arrangements for Nancy to come over, I began to follow Emily Michelle on a tour of the yard. She would bend over, inspect something, pick it up, then give it to me. We collected two rocks, a yellow leaf with black spots, an old blackened walnut that the squirrels had missed (or not wanted) and one of those little plastic tags that you stick in the ground to label plants. This one said *pansies*.

Karen and Hannie came back outside and made a beeline for a pile of wooden crates by the gardening shed. They began separating the crates, and had just finished when a car pulled into the driveway. Mr. Dawes was dropping Nancy off. Karen ran to her and led her to the shed, talking excitedly.

"Wow, *neat*," I heard Nancy say admiringly as they went by.

I followed Emily Michelle around to the back of the shed, convinced her she didn't want to inspect a partially opened bag of cow manure any more closely, and helped her collect another plant label (*sweet alyssum*). When we rounded the corner, I saw that the Three Musketeers had started stacking the crates up in two parallel lines. The back line was against the side of the shed.

"So what're you building?" I asked.

"A playhouse," said Hannie, her face red from bending over to lift the crates.

"The inside of the crates are going to be shelves," explained Karen.

"We're going to decorate the playhouse," Nancy added.

"Flowerpots!" cried Karen, and she and Nancy began to wrestle with a giant empty flowerpot at the side of the shed.

Just then David Michael careened to a stop,

holding Shannon's ball a safe distance above his head. "What kind of house are you guys building?"

I looked at David Michael with new respect. How had he known, right away, that the Three Musketeers were building a house?

"A playhouse," said Karen. She and Hannie began to wrestle the flowerpot into an upside-down position.

"You should make a fort," David Michael said.

"A playhouse," said Karen firmly.

"A fort would be better," said Linny.

"How do you know?" asked Hannie.

"Yeah," said Karen. "And besides, we're going to fix this up extra special."

"Yeah," echoed Hannie.

David Michael looked at Linny and Linny shrugged and held his hands out, palms up, and he shrugged, just like I'd seen Mr. Papadakis do.

"Just wait," said Karen. "When we're finished, everybody will want to see the most beautiful playhouse in the world."

The boys ignored the girls.

"Okay, Shannon," said David Michael. "Go out for a thirty-yard pass."

Linny began to run across the yard and soon they were all off playing keep-away from Shannon again.

Taking Emily Michelle's hand, I walked a little closer to the building site.

"Look," I told her. "This is going to be a playhouse."

Emily Michelle looked. I'm not sure what she saw.

"Can Emily Michelle and I watch you work?" I asked.

"*May* you," said Karen firmly. She is very particular about some things, like spelling and rules.

"May we?" I asked.

"Certainly," said Karen grandly.

"Great," I said. "And you know what? I think when your playhouse is finished, you should have a housewarming party and invite everyone to see it."

"What's a housewarming?" asked Karen.

"It's a party you have to celebrate a new house or home," I said. "A special new-house party."

"Okay," said Karen.

"Maybe," said Hannie.

I pulled Emily Michelle onto my lap and she leaned against me quietly. It was getting late. Soon Mom and Watson and Nannie would be back. Probably Sam and Charlie would be, too. Then it would be time for dinner and we would talk about what we'd done all day and — I smiled — we'd hear how smart Shannon was and all about Karen's new playhouse and about the Papadakises' news, too. I wondered what it would be like to be a foster kid. I didn't think it could be easy, even if you went to stay with a warm, fun family like the Papadakises.

I couldn't imagine what it would be like not to have a home, or to be between homes.

No place like home, I thought, and hugged Emily Michelle gently.

CHAPTER 2

Claudia Kishi was under her bed. Only her purple-and-white-striped stocking feet showed — sort of like when the house fell on the witch after the tornado in *The Wizard of Oz*.

Only Claudia's not a witch from Oz. She's the vice-president of the Baby-sitters Club and a major junk food fan.

"I know they're here," she said. "I know . . . ha!"

A moment later she backed out from under the bed holding a bag of yogurt raisins. From various hiding places around her room she'd also produced a bag of sourdough pretzels, a half-bag of Mallomars (we'd worked on those at the last meeting), and a box of Frosted Flakes.

"Frosted Flakes?" Dawn Schafer said, wrinkling her nose. "Claud, those are practically all sugar. And they're cereal. For breakfast."

"They're good," answered Claudia happily,

13

settling down on her bed with the yogurt raisins. "Try them."

Dawn, who was sitting on the floor next to the bed, shook her head. (Dawn is a health food fan as much as Claudia is a junk food fan.) "The pretzels," she said and, taking some, passed them to Stacey McGill.

Stacey took a couple of pretzels. She'd brought an apple with her, too. Dawn gave the apple an approving look.

"I'll try some Frosted Flakes," said Mallory. She was also sitting on the floor, along with her best friend, Jessica Ramsey.

Since I'd eaten some of the Mallomars at the last meeting, I decided to stick with them. I took one out of the bag, passed the bag to Mary Anne Spier who was sitting in the chair next to the telephone, held the Mallomar up, and said, "This meeting of the Baby-sitters Club will now come to order."

Remember I told you I was the president of a baby-sitting club? Well, it was Monday and we were at one of our regular club meetings, which we hold every Monday, Wednesday, and Friday from 5:30 until 6:00 at Claudia Kishi's house. In addition to being the BSC vice-president, Claudia is also the only member who has her own private phone line. That's important, because we use the phone a lot to schedule baby-sitting jobs.

I'm the president of the Baby-sitters Club because I thought of the idea, which came to me one night back before Mom married Watson. My mother kept calling people and calling people, trying to find a baby-sitter for David Michael, and I suddenly thought, What if Mom could make just one call and reach several baby-sitters all at once?

At the time, the baby-sitters I was thinking of were me, Mary Anne, and Claudia, since we were already doing a lot of baby-sitting. Then Claudia suggested that if three people were not enough, we could ask Stacey to join us. Stacey had just moved to Stoneybrook from New York, and she and Claudia had become friends. Stacey agreed, so with me as president, Claudia as vice-president, Mary Anne as secretary, and Stacey as treasurer, we were on our way. In fact, through hard work, good recommendations, and some advertising, we soon had more baby-sitting jobs than we could manage. That was when Dawn, who had just moved to Stoneybrook from California, became the fifth Baby-sitters Club member and the alternate officer.

But right after that Stacey had to move back to New York and we needed more baby-sitters, so Jessica Ramsey and Mallory Pike joined us as junior officers. Then Stacey's parents got divorced and she returned to Stoneybrook with her mother. (Her dad stayed in the city.) Now there are seven BSC members (who are also officers) plus two associate members, Logan Bruno (who is Mary Anne's friend *and* boyfriend) and Shannon Kilbourne, who lives across the street from me. The associate members don't attend meetings, but they are good sitters who can help us out in a pinch.

We also keep a notebook, where we each write down what happened at our jobs. That's how we stay up-to-date on what's happening with our clients. We also learn from each other's experiences. Different points of view often help solve problems that we might not be able to solve by ourselves.

Maybe that's one of the reasons we *are* such a successful club and business — we are so different from each other.

For example, Claudia Kishi is one of the most creative people I know. She's going to be an artist, and her eye for color and style shows in the way she dresses. It's always distinctive and funky. Today she was wearing purple-and-white-striped tights, Doc Martins (except she'd taken them off to sit on the bed), a short black ruffly skirt that looked like it was part of a women's Olympic figure-skater's costume, a purple cropped sweater with silver button covers on the back buttons, and a scrunchy black velvet hat decorated with purple and red velvet flowers. Claudia's Japanese-American, and with her long black hair and her perfect skin and dark eyes, she's beautiful. Still, being beautiful doesn't mean you can always wear the kinds of clothes Claudia wears. But Claudia can.

Stacey is Claud's best friend and the other Fashionable Dresser in the club. Part of that is her New York sense of style. Today she had pulled her blonde permed hair back into a complicated braid threaded with green ribbon. The ribbon matched her shoes. She was wearing silver capri pants, an oversized shirt with a green belt, a green checked short skirt, and gold leaf-shaped earrings.

Stacey always looks pulled together, partly because of her New York roots. But partly (I think) because she is diabetic which means she really has to be responsible about taking care of herself. Diabetes is a disease in which your pancreas doesn't make enough insulin, which means your blood sugar is out of control and could make you faint, or even get really sick. So Stacey has to be in charge of herself. She has to watch what she eats and even give herself an injection of insulin every day. That's why she chose pretzels from Claud's junk food collection, and also why she'd brought an apple along.

Anastasia Elizabeth McGill (that's her real

name, but you'd better call her Stacey!) is an only child. Her parents were very overprotective of her after the diabetes was discovered, even when she'd found a doctor she liked, and had proved that she could handle her illness. It took Stacey awhile to convince her parents to quit treating her like she might break.

Mary Anne Spier, the secretary of the BSC, is my best friend and although we look alike, with our brown hair and brown eyes, and we're both short (okay, okay, I'm the shortest person in my class), we have totally different personalities. I tend to speak my mind. (Some people would say I have a big mouth. I hate to admit it, but I do say things without thinking sometimes.) Mary Anne, on the other hand, is quiet and shy and sensitive. That doesn't mean you can bully her, though! Although Mary Anne is always willing to see the best in people, she's very perceptive and honest.

She's also kind of romantic. She's the first one of us to have a steady boyfriend, Logan Bruno. He's a Southerner, and Mary Anne thinks he looks just like her favorite movie star, Cam Geary. Logan is cute, but I think Bart Taylor, who coaches the Krushers' rivals, the Bashers, is even cuter. I sort of like Bart, as you might guess.

Mary Anne's mother died when she was very young, and Mr. Spier raised her *very* strictly. Like Stacey, Mary Anne had a hard time convincing her father that she was growing up, and could be trusted to be more responsible. He's still a strict father, but he doesn't make her wear little-kid clothes anymore. Plus, he allowed her to get a kitten named Tigger, and he gave Mary Anne more freedom.

Anyway, before my family moved into Watson's mansion, we lived next door to Mary Anne and her father. That was one of the reasons I didn't want to move to Watson's mansion. I *hated* the idea of not having Mary Anne next door. But we wouldn't have been next-door neighbors all that much longer anyway, because Mary Anne's father got married! And he married Dawn's mother, Mrs. Schafer. They'd both grown up in Stoneybrook, and had known each other in high school, when Mrs. Schafer was Sharon Porter. Then Sharon Porter had moved to California and met Dawn's dad and become Mrs. Schafer, and they had Dawn, and Dawn's brother Jeff. But they got divorced and Mrs. Schafer returned to Stoneybrook with Dawn and Jeff. Jeff eventually decided to go back to California to live with his father, but Dawn stayed here.

So Mary Anne, who had been an only child

suddenly had a whole new family. And she and her father moved in with the Schafers, so Dawn is not only Mary Anne's other best friend, but also her stepsister.

I have to admit, I didn't like Mary Anne's having two best friends at first. But Dawn is as nice a person inside as she is outside. What I mean is, Dawn is very striking looking, as beautiful in her own way as Claudia is. And she's a good person inside, too. So I learned to like Dawn, and to stop thinking I had to compete with her for Mary Anne's friendship.

Dawn has very long pale blonde hair, incredible blue eyes, and is tall and thin. She appears to be easy going, but she has definite boundaries. She doesn't eat red meat. She doesn't eat junk food. She has two holes pierced in each earlobe. And she loves ghost stories. Guess who lives in a haunted house? Dawn does! The old farmhouse where the newly combined Spier-Schafer family now lives has a secret passagway that leads from Dawn's room to the barn.

Although they are not blood sisters, Dawn is a little like Mary Anne in that they're both sensitive. But where Mary Anne is shy, Dawn just says what she thinks. It was hard for Dawn to leave California and move to cold, snowy Stoneybrook and hard, too, to choose between living in California with her father and Jeff, and Stoneybrook with her mother. But she worked it out, and I think she's pretty happy now.

Jessi and Mallory are junior BSC officers because they are the younger club members. Most of us are in eighth grade, but Jessi and Mallory are in sixth. In fact, we used to baby-sit for Mal, before she joined the BSC. She's a natural baby-sitter, which maybe is not surprising, since the Pike family is a large one: Mal has four younger brothers, three of them identical triplets, and three younger sisters. She has pale skin, reddish-brown hair, and she wears glasses and braces. She likes to write and draw and would like to be a children's book writer and illustrator when she grows up. Right now, she is secretary of the sixth grade class, in addition to being a junior officer in the BSC.

Mal and Jessi are not only junior members of the BSC, they're best friends, too. They have a lot in common, since they are both the oldest in their families, they both *love* horses and horse stories (especially the ones written by Marguerite Henry), and they both have pet hamsters.

But Jessi's not into writing or drawing. She wants to be a professional ballerina someday. She goes to a special dance school in Stamford, where she studies ballet several days after school, and she's already danced on stage in performances before real audiences.

Jessi's family is also new in Stoneybrook. Some of their neighbors gave them a hard time when they first moved here, because they are black. But once everyone got to know the Ramseys things settled down. Jessi has big brown eyes and black hair (and no glasses or braces)!

So you can see we're all pretty different. Which is why I think we have such a good baby-sitting club.

Right after I called the meeting to order (and finished my Mallomar), the phone rang. I picked it up. "Hello. You have reached the Baby-sitters Club," I said. The caller was Mrs. Arnold, who has eight-year-old identical twin girls. Mrs. Arnold told me when she needed a sitter, I took down the information, told Mrs. Arnold I'd call her back, and hung up the phone.

"Mrs. Arnold needs a baby-sitter for Marilyn and Carolyn Thursday afternoon from three-thirty until five-thirty."

Mary Anne flipped the pages of the BSC record book. "Mal or Stacey," she announced. "You're both free that day."

"You do it, Mal," said Stacey. "I'm already scheduled for the Papadakises on Tuesday, and the Newtons on Friday night."

"Great," said Mallory. Mallory and Jessi can't baby-sit at night, so we try to give them afternoons whenever possible.

I called Mrs. Arnold back and told her Mallory would be there Thursday afternoon. Hanging up, I remembered what the Papadakises had told us on Saturday.

"We may have a new kid to baby-sit for at the Papadakises soon," I told everyone.

"Is Mrs. Papadakis going to have a baby?" asked Mary Anne excitedly. Babies are lots of fun to sit for. We have even taken special classes in infant care.

I shook my head. "No. They're going to be a foster family."

"Wow," said Dawn. "That's a really cool thing to do."

"When?" asked Claudia.

"I don't know. They don't have a foster child yet, but they will soon."

"For how long?" asked Claudia.

"I don't know," I repeated.

Stacey said, "I saw a special program on television a little while ago about foster families. The kids who are placed in foster homes are usually only put there on a temporary basis."

"Then what happens to them?" asked Jessi.

"They go back to their original families once the problems have been solved. Or if the kids can't go back to their families, they try to find relatives who can take them."

"What if there are no relatives?" asked Mary Anne.

"The kids are put up for adoption."

"What if no one adopts them?" Mary Anne looked worried. "What then?"

"I don't know," Stacey said. "Lots of them stay foster kids until they grow up. Some of them just keep getting moved around from home to home."

"How awful," said Mary Anne indignantly.

"You know, Mary Anne," said Stacey. "According to that show, some of the foster kids were pretty tough to handle."

"It's still not right," said Mary Anne.

"No," I said. "Anyway, the Papadakises will take good care of any foster child for as long as needed."

"No matter what," agreed Claudia.

Just then the phone rang and by the time I'd finished lining up the next job we were talking about something else. But very soon I would remember what we had said — and wonder if we'd been wrong.

CHAPTER 3

I settled down at our table in the lunchroom next to Mary Anne and examined the special of the day. I gave the alleged chicken cutlet a poke with my fork.

"Artistically speaking," said Claudia, "today's lunch is an interesting color composition."

"Interesting," I mused. "That's a good word for potatoes that are gray."

"The arrangement is a sort of study in winter tones," Claudia went on. "For example, not only do you have the gray potatoes, but the brown chicken, the dark, winter-green spinach . . ."

"Spinach is good for you," Dawn murmured. "It makes you strong."

"Strong like Popeye," said Logan, sliding in beside Mary Anne. He doesn't always eat with us, but sometimes he does. Now he flexed one arm, pretending he was Popeye.

Mary Anne blushed.

Claud was on a roll. "Like, if you shellacked this lunch tray, you could hang it on a wall. What would I call it?" She tilted her head, making her long ponytail sweep over one shoulder.

"If you called it, I bet it would come," said Logan.

"Nah, it's already rolled over and played dead," said Stacey.

"Well, I don't call it lunch," I said. "But I'm hungry."

"Claud, if you do turn it into art, maybe we could donate it to the school auction and sell it to the highest bidder," suggested Logan. We all cracked up (although I swear Claud had a faraway, "artistic" look in her eyes).

Logan was talking about the auction our homeroom teachers had announced this morning. It was to raise money for new computers.

I have to admit, I hadn't exactly been listening. Actually, I'd been studying in case we had a pop quiz in math (we didn't). I'm a very organized person. I have to be, because I have a lot to do. (There was a time when I had *too* much to do, when I ran for class president, but I finally figured out that not even *I* can do everything. So I resigned and Pete Black, who was the best candidate running — besides me,

I mean — won, so it worked out okay.)

Anyway, even the most organized person needs to do a little extra studying sometimes. That's why I had taken my math book to homeroom that morning. And that's why I was staring down at my math book when I heard my homeroom teacher say, ". . . new computers for the lab."

New computers? That had gotten my attention. The computers in our lab now were ancient and slow and frustrating. Sometimes I wondered if the old electric typewriters people used to use weren't faster and more efficient.

"So the student council has decided to organize an auction to raise money for the new computers. It will be student-planned and student-run. The students will be responsible for the items donated. This is a chance for everyone to pitch in for Stoneybrook Middle School and to show some real creativity and initiative."

I had closed the math book (but I did keep my finger in it to mark my place) and listened while our homeroom teacher explained when the student council would hold the auction, and when and how the donations would be accepted.

This was a *great* idea, almost as good as starting the BSC. The idea of new computers made my fingers itch — and my brain, too.

But what would I donate to the auction? The BSC members would have some good ideas, I'd decided.

"What *are* you going to donate to the auction, Claudia?" I asked now, remembering my thoughts in homeroom.

Claudia looked up from her lunch tray, which she was still studying thoughtfully, and shrugged. "I don't know. Will the computers correct your spelling for you?"

We all had to laugh. Claudia's a terrific artist, but school in general is not her best subject. And spelling is at the top of her list of subjects she would like never to have to think about again.

"Some do," said Mary Anne. "Maybe you *could* donate a piece of your artwork, Claudia."

"Maybe," said Claudia vaguely.

Dawn finished her yogurt and unwrapped a sandwich. She folded back the wax paper in which the sandwich had been wrapped (wax paper is more environmentally safe than plastic, Dawn had told us) and picked up the sandwich.

"Sprouts and tofu?" I guessed.

"Not today," said Dawn calmly.

"You know what sprouts look like?" I asked.

"No," said Dawn. She began to eat her sandwich.

"Hairs," I said. "Little curly green hairs.

And they get caught in your teeth, too."

"A hair sandwich," said Logan. "Interesting."

"Euwww," said Mary Anne.

"Well *this* is all-natural peanut butter," said Dawn. "With honey and bananas."

I looked down at my plate. Actually, Dawn's sandwich was sounding pretty good. I gave the chicken cutlet another tentative poke.

Mary Anne said, "We can donate anything to the auction. Like antiques or flea market stuff, or even prizes like dinner for two or a makeover."

Dawn, who is in Mary Anne's homeroom, nodded. And Stacey added, "Or like those celebrity auctions in New York. You know, where you bid for dinner with a famous person, or for some really well-known stylist to cut your hair."

"Dinner with a celebrity," said Mary Anne dreamily, "like Cam Geary." (As I've mentioned before, Cam Geary is absolutely Mary Anne's most favorite star.)

Dawn said, "Or a membership in Greenpeace. Or volunteer work. You could donate that."

Mary Anne lost her "I-dream-of-Cam-Geary" look and said, "That's a great idea, Dawn!"

I was beginning to get an idea of my own, but then Claudia looked toward the table where Cokie Mason and her sidekick Grace Blume were sitting. "I wonder what they'll donate to the auction."

Stacey rolled her eyes and Dawn wrinkled her nose and I made a face (forgetting what I'd been thinking about). Only Logan and Mary Anne didn't react, Logan because he was concentrating on dessert, and Mary Anne because she's Mary Anne. Cokie Mason is world-class nasty sometimes, and Mary Anne (and I) have gotten caught by a few of her tricks, but Mary Anne is so soft-hearted that she tries to understand why Cokie is the way she is. Although not even Mary Anne has quite forgiven Cokie for some of the things she's done.

"Maybe Cokie'll bid for a makeover," suggested Dawn.

"It better be a good one," said Stacey.

"Let's brainstorm today at the BSC meeting," added Mary Anne quickly.

I started brainstorming even before the meeting, while I was baby-sitting for David Michael and Emily Michelle. What I was doing, actually, was trying to remember the almost-idea I'd had before Cokie and Grace had distracted me. But I couldn't recall what I'd been thinking about, so I took Emily outside to inspect the Three Musketeers' play-house.

The playhouse had a piece of plywood for a floor now, with two flowerpots and one box upended on it for stools and a table. An old blanket was flung across the "table" for a cloth. It was so big, though, it trailed along the floor.

"Playhouse," I told Emily, pointing at it. "Emily. Can you say playhouse?"

"Play," said Emily.

"Let's play hide-and-seek," said David Michael, who'd tagged along, insisting that he didn't have much homework to do. "I'll hide, and you and Emily can look for me."

"Okay, but you have to stay in the backyard," I said.

"If you'll count to a hundred."

"A hundred? A *hundred*? You need a whole hundred to find a hiding place?" I teased.

"Kris-ty." David Michael folded his arms. "Those are the rules."

"You're right, David Michael." I picked Emily Michelle up, walked around to the side of the house, and faced it with my eyes closed. "One," I began to count. Emily Michelle sang soft little nonsense words along with me until I reached a hundred. "Here we come, ready or not!" I cried. I whirled around and took Emily's hand.

No David Michael.

"Come on, Emily. Help me find your brother."

"Dog," said Emily.

"Shannon? You remember Shannon trying to find her ball? Good for you, Emily. We'll let Shannon out of the house. She can help us find David Michael if we can't find him by ourselves. Okay?"

That seemed to satisfy Emily Michelle.

With Emily walking beside me, we bent down to look under bushes. We peeked around the edge of the toolshed. We looked in the playhouse.

No David Michael.

"Hmmm," I said. "David Michael hid very well, Emily. Do you see him anywhere?"

Emily shook her head uncertainly.

"Well, we'll keep looking then."

But we couldn't find David Michael. I looked around the yard again. Had he somehow gotten into the toolshed, even though it was locked? Then I noticed the trash cans.

"I bet I know where he is, Emily. Come on."

But David Michael wasn't hiding in the trash cans. They were full of garbage bags.

"Bleh," I muttered at the smell.

Emily had let go of my hand and was drifting back toward the playhouse. I followed her.

"I think David Michael won hide and seek, Em. What do you think?"

"Play," said Emily. She stepped carefully onto the plywood floor, bumped against one of the stools, and fell on the blanket.

"Ooof!" said the pile of blankets.

Emily's face split into a big grin and she banged her hands happily on the blankets. "Davie! Davie!"

David Michael crawled out from under the blanket. He was grinning, his face red. "I almost fooled you!"

Emily held up her hands. "Davie!"

"Okay," said David Michael. He draped the blanket over Emily's head.

"Where's Emily Michelle? Emily Michelle!" he called loudly.

She threw back the blanket and shrieked with laughter.

"It's your turn to hide now, Kristy."

I looked around the yard. But before I spotted a good place, Linny came tearing across the lawn to us.

"He's coming. He's coming!"

"Who?" said David Michael.

"The foster kid. This afternoon!"

"You're getting a brother?" asked David Michael.

That stopped Linny, but only for a moment.

"We're not sure yet. But I bet we are. The people called today and said it would be this afternoon."

"That's great news, Linny," I said.

"Can we come over?" asked David Michael.

Linny started to nod, then stopped. "I don't know."

"It's probably not a good idea on your new brother's — or sister's — first day. We'll watch from the porch and wave, okay, Linny?"

"Okay, Kristy," said Linny breathlessly. "Listen, I have to get back." And he was gone, at top speed, across the street to his house.

"How about a snack while we wait?" I suggested. "Oatmeal cookies and milk?"

A few minutes later we'd settled on the front steps with our cookies and milk. And sure enough, not long after that, an official-looking car pulled into the Papadakises' driveway. (Well, it wasn't official-looking, exactly. But it was dark blue and square and could have been.) A woman got out of the driver's side of the car. She was tall and wore a suit and carried a purse that looked like a small briefcase (or maybe it *was* a briefcase). I couldn't tell from where we were sitting, but I thought she looked a little pinch-lipped, as if her shoes were too tight, or something was bothering her. I was pretty sure she was the kid's social worker. She started up the walk to the Papadakises', then stopped and turned around. She faced the car and made a beckoning gesture.

Nothing happened.

Finally she walked back to the car and pulled the door on the passenger side open.

Still nothing happened.

At last she leaned down and reached in. She stepped back, holding onto the hand of a child who looked about Karen's age.

"Wow!" said David Michael. "He's a boy!" He stopped and squinted, then looked at me. "Isn't he?"

The kid was dressed in jeans and a shirt and a loose sweater, with short, spiky hair slicked back on the sides, and a square chin that was being stuck out defiantly.

"I'm not sure," I said to David Michael. "I think so . . . maybe . . ."

They'd reached the front door now, which was flung open before the social worker could even ring the bell. Then Mrs. Papadakis was smiling and bending over, looking for a moment as if she were going to hug the boy or girl — who stepped quickly back.

For a moment, the three of them just stood there. Then Mrs. Papadakis straightened up, and said something to the child. The new kid folded his arms. Then the social worker said something. Suddenly the kid wheeled around and marched back toward the car. When he reached the front fender, he kept right on marching — straight over the hood of the car, up the windshield, and across the roof!

Mrs. Papadakis and the social worker looked too stunned to move. I know my mouth dropped open. The next second the new kid had leaned over, and somehow swung off the roof and in through the still-open car door. A moment later, he slid out, holding a small suitcase and a backpack. Leaving the car door open, he marched back to the house and inside, past the two women on the steps.

After a moment, they followed.

"Wow," murmured David Michael.

"You can say that again," I said.

"Wow," said David Michael.

CHAPTER 4

"Déjà Vu." It's a weird old song from a sixties LP (a record — not a CD, not a tape) that my mother and Watson listen to sometimes.

The name of this golden oldie refers to the feeling that you've been somewhere before, that whatever is happening right now is something you've experienced before. Which is the way I was feeling on a crisp, sunny Saturday afternoon, just cool enough outside for jackets. I was in the backyard, baby-sitting for Karen and Andrew and David Michael and Emily Michelle and Shannon . . .

Hadn't I been here before? Very, very recently?

Well, yes. But some things were a little different. For one thing, Nannie was at a bowling tournament instead of hitting the gardening center sales with Watson. Watson and Mom were at a flower show at the civic center, Sam and his friends had gotten up a game of football at the park, and Charlie was changing the oil on the Junk Bucket — with Andrew solemnly helping him.

For another, the crowd of baby-sittees was a little bigger. Nancy and Hannie, the other two Musketeers, were already here with Karen, carefully sorting through a collection of wallpaper and shelfpaper leftover from their families' decorating schemes of the past. Linny and David Michael had set up a row of old toy plastic milk bottles and were practicing soccer drills, dribbling the ball in and out between the bottles and trying to keep from knocking any over. Emily was standing next to me, her head turning back and forth from the wallpaper samples to the black-and-white flash of the soccer ball. And Mary Anne had just arrived to keep me company.

Lou McNally had joined us, too.

"Who's she?" Mary Anne whispered. She paused then said, "He?"

"She," I answered, "is Louisa McNally. The Papadakises' foster child."

"Wow! What's she like?"

"Mrs. Papadakis told us her father died a little while ago. She has an older brother who's with another foster family. And her mother, as far as they know, is still alive somewhere. She took off when Lou was a baby."

Mary Anne looked solemn. "Poor Louisa," she said softly, and I knew she was thinking about her own mother. Mary Anne may not remember her, but she still thinks about her and wonders what she was like.

I couldn't help but think about my father, just for a moment. He acts as if we're barely alive. But that doesn't make me feel like "poor Kristy."

I said quickly, "Yeah, well. Anyway, I don't think she'd answer to Louisa. It's just Lou."

Mary Anne tilted her head slightly and studied Louisa McNally. After a long moment, Mary Anne said, "You know, I think you're right."

Lou was short for Louisa, of course, so the mystery of the foster kid's gender was solved. But there were still plenty of other mysteries about her.

For instance, I wouldn't exactly say she'd joined us. The Three Musketeers had invited Lou to help them with their playhouse schemes, but Lou had shaken her head brusquely. Now she was standing across the backyard from Emily Michelle and Mary Anne and me, scrutinizing the noise and motion with what could only be called suspicion. She had folded her arms across her chest, wrapped a scarf around her neck almost up to her nose, and pulled a baseball hat low across her eyes.

Lou was wearing faded overalls and a red turtleneck sweater, but no jacket. I'd asked her when she'd arrived with Hannie and Linny if she wanted to borrow one of Karen's jackets.

"I don't need a jacket," she'd answered in a gravely little voice before walking stiffly across the yard to take up her position. She hadn't moved from it or spoken since. She was just an eight-year-old kid, and not very big for her age, but maybe you can see why she seemed mysterious and, well, tough.

Beside me, Emily Michelle said, "How."

I checked the scene to see what the question was about. "How?" I prompted.

"*How*," she insisted.

I looked in the direction she was looking — the playhouse. "House," I offered.

"How," agreed Emily Michelle and her head swung back toward the soccer drill.

"Ball," she said. She leaned forward, and then launched herself across the grass toward David Michael and Linny.

Mary Anne started giggling. "She is sooo cute," she said. "I love the way two-year-olds walk — like half of them is going to get there before the other half."

"A lot of times it works that way," I said, laughing, too. Then I realized that Emily wasn't slowing down. "Oh, lord."

Emily Michelle was traveling full tilt into the soccer drill.

I swooped across the yard and scooped her up before she could create a soccer drill traffic jam. "Whoa, Emily M!"

Emily's face scrunched up. "Balllel," she cried.

"Emily, they're playing with their soccer ball, see? Want me to go get one of your balls?"

Emily shook her head violently. "Balllel!"

"Or one of Shannon's? We could play ball with Shannon." (I hoped we could. Shannon, at the moment, was very involved with her special bone, which David Michael had given her to keep from rushing into the soccer drill after the ball, too.)

"Ballellll," cried Emily, going into hyper-wail.

"But Emily," Mary Anne began reasonably. Only it is unreasonable, of course, to think you can reason with a crying two-year-old.

"She means 'bottle'," a gravely voice interrupted, and I realized Lou McNally had spoken. She was standing in the same place, arms folded, only she seemed to be studying us now. My eyes met hers and she looked away.

"Bottle?" I said, as much to Lou as to Emily. The wails began to subside.

"Ballel," said Emily.

Oh. Well. "Let's ask Linny and David Michael if they'll let us have one of the milk bottles, okay?"

I didn't even have to ask. Linny, who'd heard the whole thing, bent down and scooped up the bottle at the end of his drill. He passed it to me as he dribbled the ball back to David Michael.

"The famous bottle pass," Linny intoned, flashing me a grin.

"Bravo," I said. "Thanks, guys." I put Emily Michelle down and gave her the bottle. She immediately sat on the ground and began to fill it with dirt.

Mary Anne and I exchanged glances, and then walked around the soccer drill to stand next to Lou.

"Hi," I said.

She didn't reply.

"Good call," I added. "I was sure Emily Michelle had her heart set on that soccer ball. Thanks."

Lou shrugged.

"You haven't met Mary Anne yet, have you? Lou McNally, this is Mary Anne Spier. Mary Anne is one of my friends. She's a baby-sitter, too. The secretary of the Baby-sitters Club."

"Hi, Lou," said Mary Anne, smiling at her. "I'm glad to meet you. Everyone's been excited about your coming to Stoneybrook."

That earned Mary Anne a quick sideways look, and not a particularly friendly one. In fact, it was a little unnerving.

But Mary Anne, who is very shy in some cases, didn't seem bothered at all. She can be as stubborn as she is shy.

"You know," Mary Anne persisted, "Louisa May Alcott was one of my favorite writers. Have you ever read *Little Women*? Or *Little* — "

"My name is Lou," said Lou. She didn't say it fiercely, or challengingly. She said it in a sort of no-nonsense monotone. It was pretty effective.

And I'd been right about her not wanting to be called Louisa!

"Well, Lou, welcome to Stoneybrook," said Mary Anne.

Lou shrugged. Again.

I was beginning to feel a little peeved. I opened my mouth and was (I think) about to put my foot in it by telling Lou she was being rude, when Mary Anne intervened. "It must be sort of a change, living with the Papadakises. Five people might feel like a big family."

"I don't *live* with the Papadakises," answered Lou. "It's *temporary*. They're not my family."

Just then Karen turned and waved. "Hey,

Lou!" she called. "Come on! We're going to put up wallpaper and paint the outside of our house a beautiful pink."

"Pink," muttered Lou scornfully.

"Not pink," we heard Nancy argue.

"Come help!" Karen called.

"No," said Lou.

"No, *thank you*," I couldn't help suggesting, in a firm but encouraging way (I hoped).

Lou stared at me. Her brown eyes were as flat as her voice. "Why should I thank someone for something I don't want?" she asked. Before I could answer she had turned and walked away from us.

I stood there with my mouth open. "Good grief," I finally managed to say.

"Pink?" Nancy's voice rose, carrying across the yard. "Pink is for *inside* a house. For a bedroom."

"It can be outside, too," Karen argued in her loudest outdoor voice.

Hannie, who had been riffling through the pages of a magazine, held it up. "Here's a blue house."

"Pink," said Karen stubbornly.

"Uh-oh," I said to Mary Anne.

"Maybe we better check things out," she replied.

I glanced at Emily Michelle, who so far hadn't moved and was intently filling her milk bottle for about the umpteenth time. Then Mary Anne and I approached the playhouse.

"Which do you like, pink or blue?" demanded Karen, pushing her glasses up on her nose.

Nancy said, "Kris-*teeee*. Tell Karen houses can't be pink on the outside."

"Nannie's car is pink," said Karen.

"This is *not* a car, this is a house," retorted Nancy.

"Lou!" called Mary Anne. "Lou, where are you going?"

For a moment I thought Lou had decided to run away and I had visions of tackling her and scooping her up just like I had done with Emily Michelle. Only I didn't think it would be quite as easy.

Fortunately, Lou slowed down long enough to call, "The mail just came," over her shoulder.

"I'll watch her across the street," Mary Anne said to me and followed Lou to the front yard.

They returned a minute later, Lou with her hands in her pockets, head down, shoulders scrunched up. "Sometimes they don't deliver as much mail on Saturday," I heard Mary Anne say.

Why was I not surprised when Lou didn't answer?

Lou took up her position again, and this

time, at least, David Michael looked up and said, "You want to do a drill?"

Lou shrugged, but stepped up to the soccer ball and, head still down and shoulders still hunched, but with her hands out of her pockets and balled up into fists, began to dribble the ball.

"I wonder who she's expecting a letter from," I murmured as Mary Anne rejoined me.

"Maybe her brother," suggested Mary Anne. "Or maybe her mother . . ."

"Kris-*teeee*," said Nancy.

"Right," I said. "Well. There *are* pink houses. In certain cities. And at beaches, sometimes."

"See!" cried Karen triumphantly.

I took a deep breath. "*But* Victorian houses used to be painted three or four colors. Why not have a pink and blue house? Maybe a blue house with pink trim?"

"Or a pink house with blue trim," said Hannie.

"Or . . ." began Karen, but just then the soccer ball scooted past Lou and took a long hop through the front door of the playhouse. Lou trotted over to pick it up.

"We're going to paint our house," said Nancy. "You want to help?"

"It's not even a real house," said Lou scornfully. She dropped the ball, punted it back toward David Michael and Linny, and ran after it.

Nancy looked puzzled, Karen looked indignant, and Hannie looked angry.

"What's wrong with a playhouse?" asked Nancy.

"Nothing!" said Karen loudly. "*And* we can mix blue and pink together and get . . ."

"Purple!" shouted Hannie.

"Or lavender," said Mary Anne.

"Like jelly beans," said Nancy.

"Home sweet home," I teased them. But I couldn't help thinking, just for a second, about what Lou would call a real house — and a real home.

CHAPTER 5

Sunday

Well, when I met Louisa (excuse me, Lou) McNally yesterday at Kristy's, I have to admit, I felt sorry for her. She's had a hard time, losing her father, getting separated from her brother, not knowing where her mother is or if she even cares. I know they're trying to find relatives for Lou, and I know Lou knows it, too, but still, she's just a little kid.

All that is still true, of course, but after sitting for the Thomases & Brewers & company (including Lou), I'm beginning to think she's not so shy. And maybe a lot tougher than I thought ....

It was the day after Mary Anne had met Lou at my house. I was spending that afternoon with Bart and a giant bag of popcorn at the movies, and Mary Anne was back at the "big house" sitting for David Michael, Karen, Andrew, and Emily Michelle. And the usual crowd had gathered: Linny, Hannie, Nancy — and Lou.

Mary Anne decided to give Lou a little space, so she didn't rush over and start talking to her right away. Besides, Emily Michelle was in overdrive that day, scooting around the yard with her milk bottle (again). She was also pulling a wagon, which she was filling up with anything she could find (she'd graduated from filling up the milk bottle, I guess). When she couldn't pick something up, she'd stop and look at Mary Anne. It took Mary Anne a moment or two to understand the first time, but after that, Emily Michelle had her pretty well trained.

David Michael and Linny were playing catch today. Shannon was sacked out by the door, rolled over on her back with her feet in the air. The Three Musketeers had decided their playhouse was finished and it really was time to decorate it. Mary Anne had found some old mismatched plates and cups in the barn at her house, when she and Dawn had been sifting through it looking for items for the auction, and had brought those over to donate to the playhouse.

It was, Mary Anne reflected, about the only thing of any use she'd found in the barn. Nothing in either the barn or the attic had been right for the auction. Many of the things in the barn belonged there, like the old harnesses hanging on the wall. And who would bid on old harnesses? Some of the other things in the attic — like the rickety love seat — were things that Mary Anne's dad and Dawn's mom were planning on refinishing and using in their farmhouse. And the old clothes were really ancient.

Although you never knew when old clothes were going to come in handy, thought Mary Anne, looking at the motley crew of painters at work on the playhouse. All three Musketeers were dressed in a hodgepodge of their oldest clothes, with an equally hodgepodge collection of hats. They'd just started to paint the playhouse, having at last agreed on pink with purple trim for the outside, and blue for the inside.

Karen was the first to say anything to Lou. "Hey!" she called. "Hey, Lou!"

Nancy joined in, but Hannie just kept on painting.

Lou, who had taken up position near the game of catch, finally looked over at the girls.

"We're painters," sang Karen. "Come paint the house!"

Lou shook her head vehemently. "Pink? No!"

"I like pink!" said Karen.

To Mary Anne's surprise, Lou unfolded her arms, and walked to the playhouse. (Today she was wearing her overalls under an enormous old sweater. The sweater had been patched at the elbows, and had definitely seen better days. Mary Anne wondered if maybe it had been Lou's brother's sweater, or maybe even her father's.)

"What's wrong with pink?" asked Karen.

"It's a dumb color," said Lou, and before Karen could say anything else she went on.

"Why don't you build a fort? Or a clubhouse? A *private* clubhouse. No one allowed unless you want them."

Hannie spoke up without breaking her painting stride. "Pink is not dumb and this *is* a private playhouse."

There was a little silence as the four girls stood there, Nancy and Karen with their paintbrushes lowered, staring at Lou, who was staring back at them, Hannie still painting ferociously.

"You could use the purple paint," offered Nancy. "Or the blue paint inside."

"It's a Victorian playhouse," said Karen. "We mixed the blue and the pink to make purple — "

"Lavender," said Nancy.

" — and we have exactly just enough blue left for the inside."

"Good luck," said Lou (not like she meant it, thought Mary Anne, who was sort of in shock at this more outgoing, if not necessarily more friendly version of Lou). She watched Lou return to the game of catch. The ball sailed over David Michael's head and Lou reached up, snagged it, and tossed it back to Linny. After that, she seemed to be automatically included in the game.

Mary Anne picked up a tree branch that Emily Michelle pointed to, and put it in the wagon.

Filling the wagon with found objects reminded her of the auction. A list of some of the items had already been posted on the main bulletin board as SMS and it was depressing, in a way. One student's parents had donated dinner for two at their French restaurant. Another student, whose parents ran a sporting goods store, had donated an expensive new baseball glove. And although Cokie, the queen of rude, and her crowd hadn't said what they were donating, they were dropping obnoxious hints about how impressive their donations would be.

I wish I hadn't done such a good job of clearing stuff out when I moved to Dawn's, thought Mary Anne. Then she thought of the stuff she had thrown away — one-eyed stuffed animals and old magazines with pictures of Cam Geary in them (okay, so she had cut out the pictures and saved them) and the little girl clothes her father had once made her wear. She knew she couldn't have donated those to the auction anyway.

Still, she had to come up with something to donate. But what?

Just then, Emily stopped to fill up her milk bottle with acorns.

Lou winged the ball back to David Michael and it zoomed into his glove with a *smack*.

"Oww!" said David Michael.

"Pretty good," said Linny.

"We could go down to the playground and really practice," said Lou.

"Can't," said David Michael.

"Why not?" she asked.

"Because we have to stay here with Mary Anne today."

"*Why?*" asked Lou.

"It's the rule," said David Michael.

"Well it's dumb." Lou said.

Emily Michelle emptied the acorns into the wagon and laughed delightedly at the noise they made. She bent over and began to refill her bottle.

"Rules!" Lou scooped up a grounder, and Mary Anne made a mental note to mention her softball skills the next time she saw Kristy. "They treat you guys like babies."

David Michael looked mutinous, but he didn't say anything. Yet.

"I don't believe it," Lou pressed on. She was looking at David Michael, but her words seemed, if anything, aimed more at Linny. "It's like being in jail, all the rules the Papadakises have."

"It is not," said Linny. He fumbled the ball, then got a grip on it and threw it to David Michael. Only it flew over David Michael's head again.

David Michael ran after it and Lou said, "Who ever heard of coming straight home after school? And having to sit down at meals with everybody? And nothing to eat between times. Starvation city!"

"We just can't have candy and stuff," said Linny.

"Yeah, well I hate vegetables, so I'm starving."

By now, David Michael had returned holding the ball, but he didn't throw it. "What else do they make you do?" he asked, oblivious to the darkening look on Linny's face.

Uh-oh, thought Mary Anne. Aloud she said, "Come on, Emily Michelle, let's pull your wagon over here." They began to edge toward the game of catch.

"Mr. and Mrs. Papadakis make us tell them where we're going," said Lou.

"Wow," said David Michael. (Although of course we have the exact same rule at our house.)

"And I have to show them my homework. To prove that I did it! My fath — I've *never* had to do that."

"Wow," said David Michael again. "We don't even have to do that. Just if we need help."

"But you have to *do* your homework, David Michael," said Mary Anne, who by now was close enough to intervene.

"Linny has to *show* it to his parents," said

Lou. The tone of her voice hadn't changed. It was still as flat and gravely as ever. But her words were having plenty of impact.

"So?" said Linny.

"Too bad, Linny," said Lou. "Too bad your own family doesn't trust you, Linny."

"That's not true!"

"The rules don't mean Linny's family doesn't trust him. They mean his family cares," said Mary Anne.

Abruptly, Lou took the ball out of David Michael's hands. "Come on, let's go to the playground. This is dumb." She charged toward the street.

Linny and David Michael started after her.

"Whoa!" said Mary Anne.

David Michael slowed down. But Linny and Lou didn't.

"Hey!" called Mary Anne. She strode after them, her temper starting to get the better of her. But she was also thinking, What if they don't stop? What am I going to do? It was a baby-sitting nightmare, losing complete control of one of your charges. Or, in this case, two.

"LINNY!" shouted Mary Anne.

Now as you know, Mary Anne is quiet and shy. She *never* shouts.

Maybe that's why Linny stopped in his tracks.

But Lou kept going.

Mary Anne broke into a furious run and caught Lou by the arm.

"Hold it *right* there!" she ordered.

Lou yanked against Mary Anne's grip. She was strong.

Mary Anne yanked back — only she didn't yank Lou back toward my house. She yanked her in the direction of the street.

"If you don't want to stay and play in the backyard with us, I'll be glad to walk you back to the Papadakises!"

Lou tried once again to yank free. Mary Anne kept walking.

"Wait," said Lou.

"Why should I listen to you?" asked Mary Anne. "You didn't listen to me."

"Can't you take a joke?"

"I'm not laughing," said Mary Anne. She slowed down a little.

"It was just a joke," said Lou. "Okay?"

Mary Anne stopped and turned to face Lou. Lou met her eyes defiantly. She didn't look the least bit sorry.

But then, maybe an apology was too much to expect.

"You want to go back with the other kids? And stay in the yard?" asked Mary Anne.

Lou shrugged.

"Is that yes, Lou?"

Lou shrugged again, then said, "Yeah. Sure."

"Fine," said Mary Anne. She turned around and saw Linny and David Michael. Lou tried to pull free again, but Mary Anne held on until they'd returned to the game of catch.

"Play ball," ordered Mary Anne.

Without a word, the kids spread out across the yard. Lou pitched the ball to David Michael and they started playing again.

David Michael looked guilty. Linny looked cross.

But Lou looked pleased somehow.

Mary Anne had felt sorry for Lou. But seeing her expression now, she was finding it hard to feel sorry for Louisa McNally. In fact, she was finding it hard to like anything about her.

CHAPTER 6

"That's everybody," I said as Mallory and Jessi hurried through the door of Claudia's room. I pulled my green visor down and intoned, "This meeting of the Baby-sitters Club will officially come to order."

"Order?" teased Jessi. "I'd like some pizza."

"How about some pizza puffs?" asked Claudia. She pulled out the bottom drawer of her dresser and reached into the back. "I think I have some in here . . ."

"Pizza puffs? Yeccch," Dawn said.

"Mmmph." Claudia yanked at something. She pulled out a bag, but it wasn't pizza puffs.

"Marshmallows," Dawn noted.

Claudia gave the bag an experimental squeeze. "They're still soft. If we had some graham crackers and some Hershey's bars, we could make s'mores."

"You forgot the campfire, Claud," Stacey pointed out. She was drinking a diet Coke.

"Have a Fig Newton," suggested Mary Anne, holding out the half-empty bag of Fig Newtons Claudia had unearthed earlier.

Claudia made a face. "I don't understand it," she said. "I know I had some *good* stuff around here somewhere."

Dawn said, "Fig Newtons are good. They're healthier than a lot of other snacks that have sugar and things like that in them."

"That's what I mean," said Claudia mournfully. "What happened to all my *good* stuff?"

Just then the phone rang. I picked it up. "Baby-sitters Club." I took down some information, then said, "We'll call you back, Mrs. Barrett." As I hung up, Mary Anne, her pen poised over the club notebook, said, "Wow. Mrs. Barrett. She called during a meeting."

We understood what Mary Anne meant. Mrs. Barrett is nice but she is disorganized — organizationally different, you might say — which meant, among other things, that she often forgot to call during meetings, but usually called afterwards, or on the wrong day, or something. Of course, we always tried to arrange sitters for her kids, anyway.

I nodded and said, "She needs a sitter for Buddy, Suzi, and Marnie this Friday afternoon."

"I have a class officers meeting after school," said Mal quickly. I couldn't help but smile, not only because Mal had been so sure she wouldn't win the election when she ran for secretary of the class, but also because she's taken care of the three Barrett kids before and, while she likes them, she's had her problems with them. Not for nothing had Dawn once dubbed the Barrett kids the Impossible Three.

"I'm scheduled for the Rodowskys that night," said Claudia.

Mary Anne studied the book and then said, "What about you, Jessi? It's an afternoon job."

"Okay. Great." Jessi grinned.

Business was brisk for the next few minutes, but we finally called every client back.

When things slowed down, Mary Anne suddenly said, "Speaking of ideas, has anybody thought about the auction?"

Claudia groaned. "I've been trying *not* to think about it."

"You're creative, Claud. You should be thinking about it," said Dawn.

"Somehow, I don't think my artwork is going to be a hot auction item," said Claudia. "Although someday of course, even my childhood scribblings will be enormously valuable."

Stacey grinned. "I'm saving everything you've ever made for me, just in case."

"What about art lessons?" suggested Claudia. "I could give art lessons."

"I could give ballet lessons," said Jessi.

I leaned back and stared up at the ceiling thoughtfully. "I wonder what Cokie Mason and her friends are donating?"

A little silence followed. Then Stacey said, "When you think of some of the stunts Cokie's pulled in the past . . ."

"*Mean* lessons?" said Mary Anne. Then she said, "Oops," and clapped her hand over her mouth. Which just goes to show how absolutely disgusting Cokie and her friends are, because Mary Anne never, *ever* says anything nasty about anybody, even if she deserves it. But then, Cokie mega-deserves it, in light of some of the nasty things she's done to Mary Anne in the past (attempted boyfriend theft, for one thing).

Dawn, who had been inspecting the contents label on the bag of marshmallows with a little frown on her face, pointed out, "You know, whatever Cokie and company donate, no matter how fabulous, it *is* for a good cause. So really, the better the prize, the more money for our computer lab."

"True," said Mary Anne.

"Agreed." I lowered my head and looked around the room. "So what extra-fabulous prizes can we come up with?"

Of course, the phone rang again. We made arrangements for a sitting job with the Papadakises (me, in two weeks).

62

"How is Lou doing?" asked Stacey.

"It's hard to say," I hedged. "What do you think, Mary Anne?"

"It *is* hard to say," agreed Mary Anne thoughtfully. "At first, you know, I felt sorry for her. And I still do. But . . . well, she's a lot tougher than I thought. It's probably a good thing, though. It kept her going through some pretty hard times."

Stacey said, "The Papadakises are great, and I think Lou is lucky to have them for a foster family, but from Lou's point of view, things are probably still pretty tough."

"Is she as bad as you used to think the Impossible Three were?" asked Mal.

"Uh-oh," said Dawn. "The poor Barretts. Famous all over Stoneybrook for being baaad."

"Famous!" I exclaimed. The idea I'd had in the lunchroom the day the auction was announced suddenly exploded in my brain. "That's it! Famous! Famous people!"

"Who?" said Claudia. "The Barretts?"

"No. Not the Barretts. The auction. Famous people." I took a deep breath and said, more calmly, "What about getting things from famous people — you know, like your autographed picture of Cam Geary, Mary Anne — and donating those to the auction!"

"Wow, Kristy, that's a great idea!" Mary Anne's eyes shone. Then she hesitated. "But couldn't anybody write to a famous person and get their autographed photograph?"

"Not exactly a photograph. Like something really personal."

"A guitar pick from the group Smash!" cried Jessi.

"Jazzy Prince's shirt," said Mal. "Or the blanket worn by a horse that won a Kentucky Derby." We paused, and Mal added, grinning, "Well, maybe something a famous *horse* used wouldn't work quite so well . . ."

"First we have to write a letter," I said. "We have to decide what we want to say, and explain what we want the donation for. And we have to decide who we want to write to."

Blushing, Mal said, "I could help write the letter. You know, since I like writing."

"Great, Mal. We could work on that together," I replied.

"I'll find out who to write to," volunteered Stacey. "You know, like the celebrity's agent, or whoever."

Claudia nodded. "Me, too."

"So who *are* we going to write to?" asked Jessi. She wiggled her eyebrows at Mary Anne. "Besides Cam Geary, I mean."

"Derek Masters," suggested Stacey.

Mary Anne pulled out a piece of paper. "I'll write this down."

I looked at my watch. It was about two seconds to six o'clock.

"This meeting of the Baby-sitters Club is officially — "

The phone rang one last time. It was Mrs. Prezzioso.

"Why don't you take her, Mary Anne?" suggested Dawn, after I'd told Mrs. Prezzioso we'd call her back.

"I'd like to," said Mary Anne, her pen poised above the record book. "That is, if no one else . . . ?"

Everyone nodded hastily, so Mary Anne carefully wrote down her name and the time and date, while I called Mrs. Prezzioso to let her know Mary Anne was confirmed as her sitter.

"Jenny and Andrea are cute," said Mary Anne.

"Jenny's a little fussbudget, though," I said. "Her mother keeps her so neat. Like a doll. I wonder if Andrea will be the same way?"

"Well, Andrea did win first place in the stroller division of the baby parade," Jessi pointed out.

"If I had to be that neat all the time, I'd probably grow up to be messy, just to be different," said Dawn philosophically.

"Raised like a Prezzioso, turned into a Barrett," Claudia intoned.

I thought of Lou, and said, "I wonder what makes Lou like she is? She's always pushing the limits."

"I felt that way, too, when I sat with her the other day," said Mary Anne. "She was always testing me."

"She's a daredevil, for sure," I agreed. "Yesterday she took Linny's bike, which is way too big for her anyway, and rode it down the hill at the playground without any hands."

Mary Anne winced. "How badly was she hurt?"

"She didn't fall! She made it! So then she was going to take the bike to the top of the sliding board and . . ."

"No!" exclaimed Stacey.

"Mrs. Papadakis caught her just in time. But Lou was really angry she didn't get to try it."

"That's scary. I wonder what Lou will think of next," said Mary Anne.

I thought about my upcoming sitting job with the Papadakises. "Me, too," I said. "Me, too."

CHAPTER 7

Mr. Papadakis met me at the door. "Perfect timing," he said, smiling broadly. Of course being on time is part of being a good baby-sitter, but it's always nice to hear someone say something positive. Some of our clients (I won't say who) only comment on what goes wrong, instead of what goes right. (But we know we must be doing a good job because they keep calling the BSC back.)

"Linny found the car keys," said Mrs. Papadakis, entering the hallway. Upstairs, Linny leaned over the stair railing and called down, "Three cheers for Linny Papadakis!"

"Yea, Linny!" I called up to him.

"That's just one cheer," said Linny.

Hannie's head popped up beside Linny. "Kristy! Hi! I've almost finished my homework! You want to see? We're working on dinosaurs. You pick one for spelling and arithmetic and creative writing and science. I picked a stegosaurus."

As Hannie paused to take a breath I said, "Why don't you finish your homework and I'll come up and look at it in just a few minutes."

Hannie grinned, a terrific smile like her father's. "Okay!"

Linny said, "You owe me two more cheers!" He disappeared in the direction of his room and Mrs. Papadakis laughed as she began pulling on her coat.

"I'll leave you to the cheering, Kristy," she said.

And Mr. Papadakis added, "Linny, Hannie, and Lou all have homework that needs to be finished and checked. No TV until then."

"And I just put Sari down for the night. She went right to sleep." That was Mrs. Papadakis.

"And there's a snack." (Mr. Papadakis).

"Apple cake." (Mrs. Papadakis).

"The number of the Performance Arts Center is by the telephone," concluded Mr. Papadakis.

"Sounds great," I said, and I meant it. The Papadakises are *so* thorough. It's another reason they're one of my favorite families to babysit for.

We all smiled at each other, then Mr. Papadakis cleared his throat. "Okay, we'll be off. Don't hesitate to call."

"Don't worry," I said. "Have a good time."

But as I closed the door behind them I have to admit I felt a little niggling worry of my own. "Don't hesitate to call?" The Papadakises are thorough, but that didn't sound like them. In fact, it sounded as if they were expecting trouble.

The moment I thought of trouble, my mind jumped to Lou.

Stop that, Kristy, I told myself. But I couldn't help remembering Mary Anne's experience with Lou. It hadn't been outrageous or terrible. But it hadn't been pleasant.

I pushed my negative thoughts firmly aside and headed upstairs. Sari was sound asleep in her room, with her behind in the air. She was clutching a red stuffed dog by one ear. I tucked the covers a little more snuggly around them both, then tiptoed out.

I found Linny sprawled on the floor of his room reading, his pen in his hand and a notebook open beside him. "How's it going?" I asked.

He looked up at me glumly. "We have a substitute teacher and she gave us this really dumb weekly assignment."

"How dumb?" I asked.

"We each had to pick a state and write a

report on it. I picked Rhode Island."

I raised my eyebrows. "Rhode Island?"

"It's the *littlest*."

I waited. Linny sighed and explained, "I thought it would be the easiest, at least. But it's got all the same stuff the other states have. You know, produce and weather patterns and everything."

"Oh," I said. I suddenly remembered picking the shortest books for book reports when I was a kid (okay, so I still do it if I'm pushed for time) and I bit my lip to keep from smiling. "You know, Linny, sometimes I pick the shortest book for book reports, but the shortest book isn't always the easiest. In fact sometimes the things that look the easiest are the most complicated. Like *The Old Man and the Sea* by Ernest Hemingway?" My voice trailed off. Linny was looking confused. "Anyway, appearances can be deceiving."

"No kidding." Linny went back to frowning at the book open in front of him.

"So what's the state bird?" I asked jokingly. "One of those chickens?"

Linny stared at me. "How did you know?"

"It is? A chicken?"

"A Rhode Island Red. Look." He showed me the picture. It was definitely a chicken. "What else do you know about Rhode Island?" Did Linny think I was holding out on him?

70

"I was just guessing," I reassured him hastily.

"Oh."

"We'll play Monopoly when you're through," I said.

He smiled. A little. "Okay."

"Call me if you need anything."

"Does Rhode Island have a state tree?"

" 'Bye Linny," I answered.

"Kristy! Hi!" Hannie was waiting for me by the door of her room. "Look, my homework is all done!" She was waving around a notebook with a construction paper cutout of a stegosaurus on the front.

"A stegosaurus," I said.

"That's right." Hannie nodded, with a big smile on her face. Then she began to turn the pages of her notebook, explaining each one to me. In the front were her dinosaur facts. They were followed by pages for spelling and arithmetic and writing and even art, all centered around dinosaurs in general and the stegosaurus in particular.

I stopped at the art. "Um, Hannie? I'm not sure dinosaurs were *purple*."

Hannie looked up at me and said very seriously, "Ms. Colman said no one knows for sure what color they were. So they *might* have been purple."

"Oh." Hannie had a point. "Well, it looks

good. You've done a terrific job. So, you want to play a game of Monopoly as soon as Linny and Lou finish their homework?"

"I'll go set it up," Hannie replied instantly. "I'm going to be purple this time." (The Papadakises have this *ancient* Monopoly set, with colored wooden pieces. I think it was Mrs. Papadakis's when she was a kid. Really.)

Hannie bounced out of the room and I continued down the hall to see how Lou was doing.

I'd half expected the door to be closed, but it was partway open. I knocked and called through the opening, "Lou? It's Kristy."

"I know," said Lou tonelessly.

Taking that as an invitation, I pushed the door open.

I hadn't seen Lou's room before. I don't know what I expected, but I was surprised. It was absolutely, *totally* neat. The walls were a soft blue, and the comforter on the bed was a darker blue. A colorful rag rug was on the floor. A white desk and chair stood next to the bed, and on the desk stood a blue gooseneck lamp. Clown bookends held a dictionary on the desk. Blue and white chintz curtains with little yellow flowers hung at the windows. The room looked cheerful — but empty. Only it wasn't.

Lou was lying on her back on the bed with

her feet propped up on the headboard. Her shoes were neatly lined up on the rug beside the bed.

"How's the homework coming?" I asked. (Oh, lord, I sounded like somebody's mother!)

"Fine," said Lou.

"You want me to check it for you? We're going to play Monopoly after everyone's done."

"Monopoly!" repeated Lou scornfully.

I ignored her tone and said, "Hannie's downstairs setting up. She's already claimed the purple piece. You want to put any dibs in now?"

"It doesn't matter."

"Well, let me know when you want me to check your homework," I said.

Lou didn't answer as I walked out of the room.

Hannie had set up the Monopoly board on the game table in the den by the time I went downstairs. A few minutes later, as we were counting out the money, Linny called from over the stair railing, "I finished my homework."

And he had. (The state tree of Rhode Island is a red maple, in case you're interested. The flower is a violet and the motto is "Hope.")

"Yea, Linny!" I said.

"You still owe me a cheer." Linny shot out

of the room in the direction of the den.

"I'll be right down," I said to his departing back. "I'm just going to see how Lou is doing."

Lou hadn't moved from her place on the bed.

I knocked and stuck my head around the half-open door. "Hi, Lou."

"What do you want?"

"We're about to start the Monopoly game. You ready?"

Slowly Lou swung her feet off the bed, pulled on her sneakers, and stood up. She started past me out the door.

"Whoa," I said, laying my hand on her shoulder. She stiffened and jerked back.

"Let go of me!"

"Sorry. But I need to check your homework first."

Lou lowered her head and glared at me from under her brows. "What is this, prison? I'm old enough to do my own homework."

Keeping my voice as neutral as I could, I replied, "I know. But I still need to see it. It's a Papadakis family rule."

"My *name*," said Lou gratingly, "is Lou *McNally*, not Lou Papadakis."

"I still need to see your homework."

"Forget it." Lou turned around, stomped back to her bed, and flopped down on it.

"We'd like you to play with us," I told her.

Lou stared stonily up at the ceiling.

"Kris-teeee!" shouted Hannie.

Lou scowled. "The babies are calling you," she said to the ceiling.

"I hope you'll join us soon."

Lou didn't answer.

We were deep into killer Monopoly when she appeared in the doorway of the den.

"A gazzillion dollars, Kristy!" Hannie was singing. "You owe me a gazzillion dollars!"

"That rent seems a little steep to me," I teased. "Especially for Baltic Avenue. Maybe I could write you a check?"

"Cash only," said Lou in her deep, gravely voice. "Never go in debt. No credit."

Were those some of the McNally family rules? I wondered sadly.

"Hi, Lou," said Hannie. "I'm winning."

"Hey, wait a minute!" exclaimed Linny indignantly.

"Did you finish your homework?" I asked.

Lou narrowed her eyes at me, but she nodded. "It's on my desk."

It was, a neat stack of papers, meticulously written out. I had a feeling it had been finished much earlier.

But I only said, "Good work, Lou," as I returned to the den.

One look at the three stormy faces before me and I knew I'd gotten back just in time.

"We don't have to start over, do we, Kristy?" asked Hannie.

"You've already bought all the good stuff," interjected Lou. "How am I supposed to play if you already own everything?"

"It's your own fault," said Linny.

I looked at him in surprise. That didn't sound like Linny.

"You're the one who needs a *baby*-sitter to check your homework," Lou shot back. "Baby."

"Who are you calling a baby?" sputtered Linny.

"You," said Lou. *"Baby."*

"Oh, yeah?" Linny pushed his chair back and leaped to his feet.

I took a deep breath and slapped my hand down on the table so hard the houses on the Monopoly board jumped. *"Quiet!"*

Hannie's mouth dropped open and Linny's eyes widened in surprise. I had never, ever raised my voice like that with them before.

It surprised me, too. I wanted to say to Lou, Look what you made me do.

But Lou looked bored.

"Sit down, Linny," I said. "Lou, sit in my place. You can take over for me and I'll keep the bank. It was my turn to roll."

Linny sat down and Lou took my seat across from him. She looked at my stack of Monopoly money and property deeds. "You're not doing too good, are you, Kristy?"

Her eyes met mine. Then she picked up the dice. "Lucky for you I came along, before you lost."

"I was doing fine," I said before I could stop myself.

Lou smirked. "Uh-huh."

Lou won the Monopoly game (despite the fact that nothing could convince her to trade her houses for hotels, insisting that she'd rather have four houses on each property instead of one dumb old hotel) and she was, to my surprise, a pretty good winner.

We had a post-Monopoly party of milk and apple cake in a state of relative calm. Everyone went to bed without protest, although Lou muttered something about "baby hours" that the rest of us ignored.

It was nearly time for the Papadakises to return. I checked on Sari one more time, reminded Linny that he had to turn his reading light off in ten minutes, tucked Hannie in, and went down the hall to check on Lou.

She had put her pjs on, and was sitting on the edge of the bed near the window in the dark, staring out at the night. "My father never made me go to bed until I was ready," she said as I came in.

I opened my mouth — and shut it again.

Lou had not mentioned her father before.

"He sounds pretty neat," I said softly.

Lou nodded, still staring out the window. "He knew everything."

"Like what?" I sat down carefully on the bed near her. She didn't seem to notice.

"Stuff." She shrugged.

I waited.

"Sometimes . . . sometimes we'd go for night walks. He taught me about the Big Dipper and Orion. He could hoot like an owl. Sometimes an owl would answer him."

"Can you do that, too?"

"He was teaching me when . . . " her voice trailed off. Then she said, "There was a park, too. It had a stream. Once we snuck there at night, when the moon was full. We went wading. It was summer, but the water was cold. There were fireflies. Jay and I — " She stopped abruptly, then swung her feet up on the bed.

I pulled the covers down for her. Lou didn't seem to notice. It was hard to see her expression by the light coming through the door from the hall.

"You know, Lou, my father left us when I was little. He lives in California now and I — we — hardly ever hear from him. It was hard at first, but now it's not so bad."

"He didn't like you?" asked Lou.

I bit my lip. "I think he loves me and my brothers, but he just doesn't know how to show it. Maybe."

"My mother didn't love me." Lou's voice hardened. "She left and never came back. Just like my father."

I smoothed the covers, trying to understand what Lou was thinking and feeling. "Do you remember your mother?"

I didn't think Lou would answer, but she did. She said, unexpectedly, "She smelled good. And she was strong. I remember she carried me and my stroller all the way up the stairs."

"I think she loved you," I said.

Lou was silent. Then she said, "Do you think they'll find her? And that she'll want us now?"

"Oh, Lou." Impulsively, I reached out toward her.

But Lou jerked away. "It doesn't matter. I don't love *her*. I don't love anybody. Not even Jay. He can go and live with another family and forget all about me, too."

"Lou," I said.

She flung herself to the far side of the bed. "Go away."

"Lou."

"Go away or I'll scream!"

"Lou."

She put her hands over her ears and began to scream.

I wanted to pick her up and hug her and tell her it would be okay. But why would she believe me? And how would I know if I was telling the truth?

"Okay, okay!" I stood up and crossed to the door of the room. *"Okay."*

Lou stopped screaming.

"Good night, Lou."

She didn't answer.

I lay awake a long time that night in my own bed, thinking about Lou McNally. She was the most prickly, maddening kid I had ever met. But somehow, in some ways, looking at her was like looking in a mirror. We'd never been so poor and hard up as Lou and her family. We'd been lucky. I'd been lucky. But things might have been different. And if they had, I couldn't help but wonder if I might have turned out just like Lou.

CHAPTER 8

Thursday

Do you remember
when you were
a little kid how
you always thought
that you'd never
grow up (I know,
I know, I still
feel the same way)
and that everything
that the big
kids did was
automatically
super neat and
interesting? Well
Margaret and
Sophie Craine feel
the same way.
(I don't know if

Katie does, since she's only 2½). They thought going to visit the playground at Stoneybrook Middle School was The Most Excellent Adventure ...

Margaret and Sophie and Katie have a great collection of toys, not to mention plenty of imagination to go along with the toys. So Jessi was a little surprised when Margaret pushed her *Anti-Coloring Book* away and said, "I don't want to do this anymore."

"Me, either," said Sophie, who's four.

"But you're not coloring, Sophie," Jessi pointed out. Sophie looked down at the puzzle piece clutched in one hand and then dropped it back in with the rest of the puzzles. "I don't want to," she repeated stubbornly.

At that point Katie joined in, waving her terry cloth chicken over her head by one leg and shouting, "NO, NO, NO!"

Uh-oh, thought Jessi. Everything had been rolling along in a pretty predictable way until then. Jessi had arrived at the Craines' to find Margaret and Sophie busily working at the kitchen table, and Katie contentedly making stacks of blocks in her playpen — and then knocking them down. Mrs. Craine had put snacks in the fridge for later, and her list of emergency numbers along with the number where she could be reached were posted by the phone. The girls watched calmly as their mother waved and hurried out the kitchen door. Katie had even added a cheerful " 'Bye-'bye!"

But now, suddenly, they were bored.

"Okay," said Jessi. "We'll put these things away, and try something else. You want to play with your Cabbage Patch babies?"

Margaret frowned.

Sophie frowned.

Katie said cheerfully, *"NO, NO."*

"No, huh?" Jessi looked around for an idea, but nothing came to mind. And she hadn't brought her Kid-Kit with her this time, because the last time a BSC member (Mallory) had taken care of the Craine kids, she'd brought *her* Kid-Kit. We don't like to take those every time because then the kids won't think they're as special and might get, well — bored.

Which is what the Craine kids were now.

"We could go get ice cream!" suggested Margaret.

"Ice cream!" echoed Sophie.

"You have a snack for later on," said Jessi. "I don't think your mother is going to want you to have ice cream, too."

Sophie's lower lip stuck out in the beginnings of a classic pout.

Think, Jessi told herself. I am an experienced member in good standing of the Baby-sitters Club. I should be able to handle a mass attack of boredom. Still looking around for inspiration, Jessi realized that it was a beautiful afternoon outside.

"Why don't we take a walk?" she suggested.

Margaret looked thoughtful. Sophie, pulling her lower lip in, nodded slowly. "Okay. But let's go someplace good."

What does that mean? thought Jessi. "We could walk to Stoneybrook Middle School," she suggested tentatively.

"Oooh, the *big* school!" exclaimed Margaret.

Whew, thought Jessi.

SMS wasn't far from where the Craines lived, but Jessi made the walk into an expedition by getting out the wagon. The girls took turns riding in it (except Jessi) until they reached the school.

"Wow," said Margaret, tilting her head back to stare up at the second floor windows.

"Oooh," said Sophie, just staring.

"It's *big*," said Margaret.

"No!" shouted Katie.

"It is, too, Katie," said Sophie.

Jessi stared at Stoneybrook Middle School. She saw a plain old two-story red brick building. Then she tried to remember how SMS had looked the first time she'd seen it. She had to admit, it had seemed a little daunting. But that had been because she was new and was worried about all the being-the-new-girl-at-school stuff, like will I have any friends, and what if I get lost and have to walk into class late and everyone stares at me?

Jessi had a feeling that wasn't what Margaret and Sophie were thinking about. "We'll go around back," she told them.

"Is that where the playground is?" asked Sophie.

"N-no. Not exactly. We have a track, with a football field in the middle."

"Oh," said Sophie, puzzled.

But when they reached the track, Sophie's eyes widened. "It's *big*, Jessi."

"The track is a quarter mile all the way around," replied Jessi. "That is pretty big."

"Do you run around it?" Margaret asked Jessi.

"Sometimes. But I'm no track star."

"May I run around the track?" asked Sophie.

"Sure," said Jessi.

So Sophie took off, but she kept looking back, as if to make sure Jessi were still there.

Jessi, meanwhile, had pulled the wagon and Katie over the grass strip between the track and the bleachers, and had climbed up to sit on the second row. Margaret sat beside her. Katie stayed in the wagon for a moment, intently studying the bleachers. Then she clambered out and stood facing Margaret and Jessi.

"Up," said Katie and carefully begin to climb the bleachers. When she reached Jessi and Margaret she announced, "Down," and climbed back down again.

"Good, Katie," said Jessi.

"Up," said Katie, ignoring her and starting all over again.

"Jessi! Hey, Jessi!" Sophie, who was about a quarter of the way around the track, waved wildly.

"Hi, Sophie!" Jessi and Margaret waved back. Satisfied, Sophie returned to her running.

"This is a big playground," said Margaret.

Hiding a smile, Jessi agreed.

"Do you have recess here?"

"Well, not recess exactly. It's called physical education class. PE."

Wrinkling her brow, Margaret thought about this, then said, "Do you play games?"

"Down," said Katie and started her descent.

"Some," Jessi said. "Volleyball, soccer, depending on what time of year it is, and what you're good at."

"Kickball?" asked Margaret hopefully.

"No, we don't get to play kickball."

"Keep away?"

"No, although I guess some games, like basketball and soccer, *are* sort of like that."

"Simon Says?" suggested Margaret.

"Not that either," Jessi told her.

Sophie was halfway around the track now, trotting sturdily along.

"Oh." Margaret looked around and then said consolingly, "But your school is nice and big."

"Up," said Katie.

"Yes it is," said Jessi.

Sophie looked up and waved again. Then she veered off the track and began trotting across the grass toward them. She was huffing and puffing and her cheeks were red by the time she reached the bleachers.

"You ran a long way," said Jessi.

Sophie nodded, panting.

"I'll tell you what, let's go get some water at the fountain and then I'll show you something special." Jessi had just remembered that all of the donations for the auction were being stored in an old classroom at the back of SMS. We'd been keeping an eye on it (and an eye on the mailbox to see what might come in) so Jessi knew it was a pretty good collection, even if some of the things were a little weird (like the set of snow tires someone's mother had donated).

The room was even fuller than Jessi remembered. She heaved Katie up to her shoulder so Katie could see, while Margaret and Sophie stood on the wagon next to her. They peered through the window.

"People gave stuff to Stoneybrook Middle School so we can sell it to raise money for new computers," Jessi explained.

"Mom has a computer," said Margaret. "We can't play with it."

"Well, thanks to the auction, by the time you go to Stoneybrook Middle School, there will be enough computers for everyone," Jessi told her.

Margaret nodded seriously, looking impressed.

"What's that?" Sophie pointed at a shadowy figure leaning against a blackboard. For a moment Jessi was startled, then she grinned. "That's a dressmaker's dummy. When you're making a dress or something, you can try it on the dummy first."

"Look," said Margaret.

"Wow, it's an old record player, the kind you have to wind up. A phonograph. That must be an antique," said Jessi.

"Look, pretty," Katie said. She was pointing to a bear claw patchwork quilt that had been draped across the desk.

They saw plenty of other things, too, bicycles and clothes and lamps and books and all kinds of furniture. And they had fun looking at it, and trying to guess who might have donated what.

As they were heading back home, Margaret said, "What was yours, Jessi?"

"You mean, what did I donate for the auction? Nothing yet."

"Aren't you giving anything?"

"Of course. The whole Baby-sitters Club — "

"Mallory, too?" asked Sophie.

"Mallory, too," said Jessi. "We're asking famous people to give us stuff, and autograph it, even. That's what we're giving."

Margaret looked doubtful.

"Is Big Bird coming?" said Sophie, thinking of the most famous person she knew.

"Famous people aren't coming," Jessi explained. "They're just giving us stuff to sell."

"I think you should ask Big Bird," said Sophie, skipping ahead.

Jessi sighed. There was so much neat stuff in the room already. And the members of the BSC hadn't heard one word from any of the celebrities to whom they had written.

We wrote to busy people, Jessi reminded herself. It's just going to take a little time. She smiled, thinking of some of the possibilities — pretty amazing possibilities, even if they hadn't written to Baryshnikov to ask for a pair of his ballet slippers, as she had suggested.

Awesome, she told herself. When those celebrity donations start pouring in, it is going to be absolutely awesome.

CHAPTER 9

"Have you *seen* it?" I demanded, running up behind Mary Anne at her locker.

Mary Anne gave a little yelp and dropped a book. "Kristy! You scared me."

"Sorry," I said ruefully, picking up the book and giving it back to her. "But this is extremely urgent. Critical. An emergency."

"An emergency meeting of the BSC?" asked Mary Anne, her voice a little muffled as she bent back into her locker.

"No. Well, not yet, anyway. But it's important." I began to drag Mary Anne down the hall.

"What is it? It's almost lunchtime."

"Believe me, lunch will wait," I told her. "Consider how long some of that food has been waiting around the cafeteria already."

"Kristy!" exclaimed Mary Anne indignantly.

I kept pushing through the crowded hall. We were going against the traffic, because almost everyone else was headed for the lunchroom, and more than one person glared at me.

But this really was important.

When we reached the old classroom where the auction donations were being stored, I dropped Mary Anne's arm.

"Hello." Ms. Garcia, from the principal's office, was sitting behind a table by the door. "You have a donation?"

"Not yet, Ms. Garcia. We just wanted to look."

Ms. Garcia nodded, smiling. "It's quite an impressive collection. Everyone has gone all out."

"Some people," I muttered, "have gone *too* far."

Mary Anne was staring at me as if I were truly crazy, but she followed me into the classroom without saying so aloud. She's a true friend.

"The things people donate are amazing," she said, surveying the room. I told you Mary Anne never says anything bad about anybody. That was her way of saying some of the stuff was pretty weird.

Aloud I said, "Some of this stuff *is* pretty weird. And some of it is, well, outstanding."

Mary Anne stopped and ran her hand over a wooden carousel horse. "This is awesome,

Kristy. I think some of these things are *real* antiques."

"Yeah, well look at this!" I pointed dramatically.

Mary Anne looked in the direction I was pointing — at a table with several things on it. "The toaster?" she asked. "What about it?"

"Not the toaster, Mary Anne. This." I picked up a small framed certificate and practically stuck it under her nose. "Can you believe it?"

Taking the certificate out of my hands, Mary Anne held it little further away and read it.

"Wow," she breathed. "This is . . . outstanding."

It was a certificate for an unlimited three-minute shopping spree at Power Records in the mall. *UNLIMITED* it said in big gold letters, and then in case the reader didn't get the point, it said, *Bearer is entitled to collect as many compact discs, tapes, audiovisual recordings, laser discs, and videotapes, by any company, within a three minute period, in the above listed store, the time to be prearranged by mutual agreement between the bearer and Power Records Inc.*

Taped to the outside of the frame was a small notice: "Donated by Cokie Mason."

Mary Anne frowned. "Oh, no."

"Oh, yes."

"Well it *is* a wonderful donation."

"Yeah," I said glumly. "Cokie's already made a thousand remarks about what we're donating. You know what she said to me yesterday morning?" I stuck my nose in the air and tried to imitate Cokie's whining drawl. "What are *you* donating, Kristy? A Baby-sitters Club Special Award?"

Mary Anne shook her head, and started herding me back out the door and toward the lunchroom.

"I can't stand it," I said. "I mean, I don't want to compete with Cokie. This isn't about competing, it's about helping the school have a real, up-to-date computer lab . . ."

". . . but it's hard not to," Mary Anne finished for me. "I know, Kristy. But your idea was a great one. And as soon as the celebrity donations start coming in, we'll be all set."

"If they come in," I said glumly.

We filled our lunch trays and sat down at our table. I have to admit, I was so depressed it was hard to think of something truly gross to say about what the cafeteria was dishing up. I ate the "sea legs special" with the strange pink tartar sauce, while Mary Anne told Claudia and Stacey and Dawn about Cokie's donation.

"Don't worry," replied Claudia cheerfully. "We've got it covered. Right, Kristy?"

"Mmf," I said, around a mouthful of fish.

"I can hardly wait to see what Cam Geary sends us," said Mary Anne.

"Or Sweet Jane," added Stacey. (She's the lead singer of a New York club group called the Sleazebuckets. Some people around here really like them. The high school kids make special trips to New York just to hang out in the clubs and listen to them. Stacey assured us we'd need to include them on our stars donation list.)

"You know, all kinds of things in the sea have legs. What kind of legs do you think these really are?" I asked.

"Kristy. Gross," said Stacey.

"Sorry," I said contritely. "Well, anyway, I think we better have a Plan B to fall back on for this auction."

"What's Plan B?" asked Dawn.

"We comb our houses and attics after all. See if we can find some really good stuff stuck away."

Mary Anne looked doubtful. "Dad and I did a lot of cleaning up and throwing away before we moved in with Dawn."

"We did some pretty mean cleaning before you moved in, too," replied Dawn, smiling.

"You never know," I said. "It can't hurt to look."

Ouch. I was wrong. Because just then I

glanced up — and Cokie and Grace were walking by. "This auction is so exciting, don't you think?" said Grace, pausing to smile her phony smile at us.

"Thrilling," I answered flatly.

"It'll be a real *record* breaker," said Cokie. "I've seen to that."

"Really?" said Dawn.

"But maybe you haven't seen *my* donation to the auction," Cokie went on.

"It's *fabulous*," breathed Grace.

"You'll see it when you take your little donation down. I'm sure you'll find *some*thing to donate," added Cokie. She smiled, a smile about as warm as winter in Alaska. "Ta," she said and strolled away.

I grimaced. But I was determined. Saturday was going to be the great attic search at my house, and I was going to find something terrific if it killed me.

Saturday was part of a "big-house" weekend. That meant that Karen and Andrew were staying over.

"Guess what?" I said at breakfast.

I should have remembered not to say that. Karen can be very literal-minded sometimes.

"You are going on a long, long trip?" she suggested.

"No, I . . ."

"You are going to meet a tall, dark stranger?"

"I'm not . . ."

"You might," said Karen.

"I'm going on a treasure hunt," I told her.

"Can I come, too?"

"Me too, me too," cried David Michael.

"And me," said Andrew.

"Me," echoed Emily Michelle.

"In the attic," I said. "Right after breakfast. For stuff for the auction." (I'd already told everyone about the auction.)

"The attic." Karen opened her eyes very wide. "Oooh. Maybe Ben Brewer is waiting . . ."

"Ben Brewer?" Andrew looked worried.

"Ben Brewer is *not* waiting," I said firmly. Karen believes the ghost of Ben Brewer, who was her great-great-grandfather, still haunts his bedroom on the third floor.

Even David Michael looked a little concerned. But he said, "Why would Ben Brewer leave his bedroom?"

"Because he doesn't want us taking something that belongs to him. He wants it to stay in the attic." Karen lowered her voice dramatically. *"Always."*

"Ben Brewer is not going to leave his bedroom," I said.

"Ben Brewer's in his bedroom?" Andrew's eyes grew even bigger than Karen's.

"No!" I said hastily. "There is not a ghost! Okay?"

"I'm not going," said Andrew firmly.

Nannie, who had just come in to pour herself a cup of coffee, said, "Then maybe you can help Emily Michelle and me in the garden this morning, Andrew."

Andrew didn't even ask what Nannie wanted help with. He just nodded vigorously.

So right after breakfast, David Michael, Karen, and I headed up to the attic.

Creeakkk. The third floor landing above us made a noise as we began climbing the stairs from the second floor to the third floor.

Karen stopped. "Ben Brewer," she whispered.

"It isn't Ben Brewer," I said.

Neither Karen nor David Michael looked convinced. "All right, I'll show you."

I took a deep breath. "Ben Brewer! Come out!"

Nothing happened.

"Let me try," said Karen. She made her voice deep and eerie. "Bennn Brewerrr, come out. If you don't want us to go to the attic and find your treasure, come ouuut."

Creakkk, said the landing.

"Eeeeek!" screamed Karen and David Michael.

"Arrrgh," I said, trying not to scream.

And Boo-Boo, Watson's fat, bad-tempered old cat, thumped past us.

We stood open-mouthed, watching him until he disappeared down the stairs. Then David Michael started to laugh. "If Ben Brewer is there, I bet Boo-Boo scared him away."

"Boo! Boo! Ben Brewer," said Karen.

After that we reached the attic without any more scares.

The attic is a neat place (well, not neat — it's dusty and jumbled full of furniture and all kinds of stuff that people couldn't quite bring themselves to throw away, like big, heavy old wooden tennis rackets, and chairs without seats in them). The light comes in through a narrow little window and when you bend over to look out of it, you can see all across the neighborhood, like in *A Little Princess*.

I turned on my flashlight and began to walk around the big old room, ducking to avoid the rafters.

"Look," said David Michael. He reached under a chair with the stuffing coming out and pulled out a dusty wooden box.

"Treasure," breathed Karen.

We knelt down and I carefully pulled the lid off.

"Newspapers," said David Michael disgustedly. And that's what was in the box. Dozens of old copies of the *Stoneybrook News*, all yellowed and crumbling. I poked through them carefully, but they turned out not to be so old after all.

"Too bad," I said, replacing the box lid. "Some old newspapers are really valuable. We'll leave these, though. Maybe in a hundred years, they'll be valuable to someone else."

"Maybe Ben Brewer likes to sit in *this chair* and read them," said Karen.

David Michael peered critically at the lumpy old chair. "It looks awfully uncomfortable. Do ghosts read, Kristy?"

"I don't know," I said. I aimed my flashlight hastily around the room to find something to distract Karen and David Michael from thoughts of Ben Brewer. "Look!"

It was a dusty old leather bag. I unzipped it and started to laugh.

"What is it?" Karen said as she and David Michael leaned over to peer in the bag.

"A pink bowling ball," I said. "Maybe it belongs to Nannie."

"Wow," said Karen. "Can we have it for our playhouse?"

"I don't see why not," I said. "We'll ask Nannie."

"What do you need that for?" said David Michael.

Karen shook her head impatiently. "It *matches*," she explained. But I don't think David Michael understood her.

We poked around for a little while longer. We found all kinds of weird and interesting things, but nothing good enough for the auction. I have to admit, at this point, I would have welcomed old Ben Brewer's ghost, if he would have helped me find something super.

But the pink bowling ball was the biggest (and heaviest) treasure we found. Nannie said, "Heavens, I'd forgotten that," when we asked her about it, and told us to do whatever we wanted with it. So that afternoon I took the bowling ball outside when Hannie and Nancy came over to work on the playhouse. The girls were suitably impressed with it.

"Gigundoly super," said Hannie.

"Super gigundoly super," said Nancy.

"Where do you want me to put it?" I asked.

"By the door," said Karen. "We will use it as a doorstop."

"You don't have a door," David Michael pointed out.

"We will," said Karen firmly. Then they set

to work decorating the "shutters" that Claudia had painted around the windows on the outside of the playhouse. They were using an assortment of flower and seashell stickers.

"Beautiful," said Karen.

"Fabuloso superoso," I said.

"Hey! Hey, David Michael!" It was Linny and Lou, crossing the backyard.

David Michael waved and trotted over to them.

To my surprise, Lou headed toward the girls and me.

"Hi, Lou," said Karen, pushing her glasses up her nose. "You want to help us?"

"With a *playhouse*? No way. It's not a real house," said Lou scornfully.

"It's fun, though." That was Hannie. She looked a little wary of Lou, but she smiled.

"Fun?" Lou retorted. "I don't think so."

"Try it," urged Nancy. "Here." She handed Lou a sheet of seashell stickers. "Pick a good one and stick it up."

Lou held the sheet of stickers awkwardly for a moment, then slowly peeled one off. She studied the shutters and I felt myself tense.

Then her eye fell on the bowling ball. She leaned over and stuck the sticker on the bowling ball. "There," she said.

"What a good idea," said Karen, bending to examine the bowling ball.

"It's a dumb bowling ball," said Lou.

"No, it's a doorstop now," said Hannie.

The Three Musketeers were being extremely nice to Lou. I was touched. But Lou wasn't. In fact, the nicer they were, the meaner she became.

"It's a stupid house with a stupid doorstop *without* a stupid door," said Lou. She turned and stomped away.

Karen, Hannie, and Nancy were quiet for a moment. Then Karen said thoughtfully, "If we had an old shower curtain, we could use it for the door and the window. Then our house would be waterproof . . ."

Lou joined the boys and I sat down nearby to scratch Shannon's chin. The sounds of the kids playing floated around me: "Faster, faster," called David Michael. "Come *on*." (Lou.) "Yea, me!" (Linny.)

And behind me, Hannie said, "This be a playhouse *and* a clubhouse. Then Lou could use it, too."

"We'd need a real door, though," said Nancy. "I think we'd need a real door. We could still use shower curtains for the windows, though."

Karen said, "Yeah. And Lou's right. If you have a doorstop, you really do need a door."

"We could make a sign, too. It could say Clubhouse and Playhouse."

"In alphabetical order," Karen agreed with Nancy.

In the street I saw the mail truck cruise by. I stood up and trotted toward the front of the house. Might as well see what celebrity items had (or more likely, hadn't) shown up.

Lou shot past me at top speed then, braked long enough to make sure no traffic was coming, then ran to the Papadakises' mailbox. She pulled out a fistful of mail and shuffled through it.

Obviously, she didn't find anything she liked. She crammed the mail back in with a scowl, slammed the box shut, and ran fiercely across the street.

I hadn't found anything either.

"Saturdays are always slow for mail," I told Lou as she sped by.

She didn't even slow down. "Who cares!" she shouted over her shoulder.

CHAPTER 10

"Have you ever noticed," asked Claudia, "that pizza is like all those weird math problems? If you have six pieces of pizza and you eat one, what's left?"

"Not enough pizza!" Jessi liberated a slice and held it up triumphantly.

"We have two pizzas," Mary Anne pointed out.

Claudia grabbed her throat in mock horror. "No, no, no! *Two* pizzas is not part of the math problem!"

"This is not a math problem, Claud, this is dinner," I said.

"You're right." Claudia grinned, picked up a slice from one pizza box, and laid a slice from the other face down on top of it. Taking a big bite, she explained, "Pizza sandwich," only it sounded like "izza unwich."

That was the signal for the feeding frenzy to begin and we divided it up while passing around the diet soda and napkins and plates. For a little while, no one talked about anything.

It was Saturday night. Watson and Mom had taken David Michael and Emily Michelle and Andrew and Karen to the movies. Nannie, Charlie, and Sam were out doing Saturday night things. And the BSC was sitting around my kitchen table finishing off two pizzas, one with everything (hold the anchovies) and one super vegetarian (everything, hold the meat *and* the anchovies).

Only two weeks were left before the auction and we had not one single thing to donate. Not a single celebrity had written back to us. And all of our searching through attics, basements, garages, and a barn hadn't turned up a single treasure worthy of donation.

We were in trouble, which is why I suggested a BSC brainstorming and sleepover party.

"Too bad we can't donate all the pizza you can eat to the auction," I said.

"How do you think Cokie convinced Power Records to donate that shopping spree?" mused Dawn for about the hundredth time.

"Her charm," said Claudia solemnly.

"Her father's connections," said Stacey.

"Everybody's talking about what a great donation it is," said Mary Anne.

I nodded glumly. "Especially Cokie and Grace. If I hear Cokie say what a *record-breaking* auction this is going to be one more time, I'll . . . I'll . . . "

"Do something fiendish to her?" suggested Mallory innocently.

"Thanks, Mal," I said, and we all cracked up.

After a moment, I realized that Claudia was staring at me intently.

"What is it?" I asked. "Did I spill something on my sweater? Do I have pizza stuff stuck in my teeth?"

"Kristy, I've decided." Claudia stood up. "I'm going to give you a makeover."

I ducked, putting my hands over my head.

Mary Anne started laughing. "It's okay, Kristy. Try it. You'll like it." (Mary Anne had had one herself recently.)

"Yeah, it'll be fun," said Jessi.

"Fun, ha!" I exclaimed, as Claudia grabbed my elbow and began to lever me out of the chair.

"We'll clean up this mess and meet you in the den," said Stacey.

"Okay," replied Claudia.

"Wait a minute," I protested.

But a few moments later I was sitting on a footstool in the den while Claudia rummaged through the contents of various makeup kits.

Dawn tucked a kitchen towel into the neck of my sweater. "Try that Body Shop lotion," she said. "It's all-vegetable."

I winced as Claudia began to rub something on my face. "It's cold."

"It's good for you," Dawn told me.

Stacey, who had finished cleaning up and was crouched down by the videos with Jessi and Mal, said, "Oh, wow, look! *The Wizard of Oz.*"

Mal groaned. "We've seen that about a million times at our house. It's one of Claire's favorites."

"I still love it," said Mary Anne.

"Me, too," Dawn said. "Except I never could watch the scary part in the beginning."

"The tornado!" cried Stacey happily, pushing the tape in. "We'll just watch the tornado part, Mal, okay?"

I smiled — and Claudia frowned. "Don't move," she warned me.

She put more goop on my face. She wiped some off. She told me not to blink. She told me to blink. She tilted my head back.

"No peeking up my nose," I said.

"Ewwww!" squealed Jessi.

"Don't talk," Claudia ordered.

Just about the time the tornado was finished with Kansas, Claudia was finished with me.

"Voilà!" she cried as the munchkins danced onto the screen in full color.

Everyone turned to stare at me.

"Don't all laugh at once," I muttered.

"It's . . . different," Dawn said.

I snatched the mirror out of Claudia's hand and stared at myself.

Claudia had made a layer of little braids in my hair, which made my ears stick out. She'd given me raspberry colored eyelids and had put mascara on my eyelashes. I looked startled. My eyebrows had been brushed up, which made me look even more surprised — which I was.

I had blush on my cheeks, and glitter shadow beneath my eyebrows and raspberry colored lips. And Claudia had painted little stars on my earlobes. As I put one finger up to touch my ear, she said, "You really need earrings, Kristy."

My big mouth that says things without thinking said, "Eeeek!"

Mary Anne said quickly, "It looks good, Claudia. It just doesn't . . . it just doesn't look like Kristy."

"How about something a little more — natural?" suggested Dawn.

"It works," said Stacey. "But . . ."

"But it's just not Kristy," finished Claudia. "I see what you mean." She sighed, then reached for the makeup. "Maybe I could . . . "

But I slid hastily away.

Just then Stacey punched the mute button on *Oz* and flipped on the radio. "Request time!"

"Maybe Curtis Shaller will dedicate a request to Jessi," said Mallory slyly.

Without hesitation, Jessi picked up a pillow and winged it at Mallory.

Mallory shrieked and whapped her back and the pillow fight was on.

Saved by a pillow, I thought, grabbing the nearest feather-filled weapon. In another second we were screaming at the top of our lungs and racing through the house.

When no one was looking, I detoured into the bathroom and gave my face a hasty wash. I figured I could say it all came off in the pillow fight, if anyone noticed. Then I returned to the game and chose a strategic position behind the sofa in the den.

I was lurking there, waiting for some unsuspecting BSC member to walk into my web and thinking, What if some of the kids we sit for could see us now?, when the words on the radio pulled me back to nasty reality.

"And this song goes out to all the generous people whose donations to the Stoneybrook Middle School Fundraising Auction will make it an *enormous* success."

Whap! "Gotcha!" shouted Mallory.

I grabbed her pillow. "Listen!"

Jessi tumbled in with Mary Anne in hot pursuit. When they saw us standing frozen in the middle of the room, they stopped.

"What's wrong?" asked Mary Anne, still holding her pillow over her head.

I nodded toward the radio and, as if on cue, the DJ, Random Dan, started his spin again. Dawn and Stacey and Claudia had run in and we listened as he said: "That's the Stoneybrook Middle School Fundraiser Auction. For you listeners who don't know what's happening, stay tuned after this tune for some of the key donations and the details of how you can give or buy something really fabulous!"

As the music kicked in, I grabbed a pencil and my notebook and said, "We have to think of something. Now!"

We sprawled around the room with our pillows.

Silence reigned.

"What about makeovers?" suggested Claudia.

I kept my big mouth shut.

Then Stacey said, "Why would you bid on a makeover when you could get one free at the cosmetics counter at a department store?"

"True," said Claudia. "But these could be really special. Personalized."

"Clown makeovers!" I exclaimed.

Fortunately, Claudia didn't take that personally. She just looked puzzled.

"We could offer a special Baby-sitters Club party, complete with clown faces for the kids," I explained.

"I like that," said Claudia.

"Another great idea, Kristy," Dawn agreed.

"What about Kid-Kits?" suggested Mary Anne. "We could make up special Kid-Kits for the auction, sort of like a mystery grab bag."

Soon we were on a roll: errand services, pet-sitting, dog walking, baby-sitting. Not all the suggestions worked (such as health food cooking for kids) but it was a pretty creative list. Enough to take the pressure off, even if we couldn't match Cokie's donation. Enough so we didn't feel guilty about goofing around and eating tons of junk food the rest of the night before crashing somewhere in the middle of the late, late, late horror movie.

Sunday morning was gray and chilly. We were all burrowed deep into sleeping bags and pretty happy about it — but in a house like mine, noise has a way of finding you no matter what. I gave in (and up) at noon when Karen answered the front door and let Hannie, Linny, and Lou in.

Nannie, who was standing in the kitchen

holding a bowl, nodded briskly when we came in. She is a morning person, so, since it was already afternoon, she was really awake.

"Hi, Nannie," I said, foraging in the cupboards with Mary Anne while everyone draped themselves sleepily around the kitchen.

"We made chocolate-covered popcorn," Claudia explained, gesturing at the bowl Nannie was holding.

"Oh," said Nannie.

"And we left the dirty pan to soak," added Jessi. "I guess we forgot to put the water in it."

"Interesting texture and patterns," murmured Claudia taking the bowl from Nannie.

"Looks like snails have been crawling in it, if you ask me," Mallory said.

Mary Anne made an "eww gross" noise and I took the bowl from Claudia, squirted some liquid soap in it, and filled it with water.

Shaking her head and smiling, Nannie fixed herself a cup of coffee and left the kitchen to us.

As Mary Anne and I put out cereal and bowls and milk the house was quiet — for about thirty seconds.

"Eeeeeeeeeeeek!"

I jumped about twenty feet. "Karen?" I gasped. But before I could do anything I heard

113

David Michael shout, "Ha, you're it!"

"Ohh." I sank down in a chair. Claudia started to giggle. A moment later, when Andrew burst into the kitchen, looked wildly around and then dove into the pantry, she went off into gales of laughter. By the time Karen came charging in a minute later, we were all laughing helplessly.

"HIII! What's so funny?" she shouted.

"Indoor voice," I answered automatically.

"*Hiii*," she stage-whispered. "Has anybody seen Andrew?"

"No fair asking," came Andrew's voice from the pantry.

Karen's eyes grew large behind her glasses. Then she leaped across the room, threw the pantry door open, tagged Andrew, and shouted, "You're it!"

She tore out and Andrew, after a stunned moment, ran after her panting, "Not fair, not fair!"

"Nofe air," murmured Dawn, raising her eyebrows at Mallory, whose little sister Claire pitches temper tantrums, shouting "No fair, no fair!" — until the words sound like "Nofe air."

We started laughing all over again.

"How does anyone have so much energy so early in the day," said Claudia weakly.

"We did stay up most of the night," Stacey pointed out.

"True," agreed Claudia. "Working on auction ideas."

"And gross food combinations," said Jessi. "Like chocolate popcorn."

"And Fritos dipped in butterscotch pudding." Mallory made a face.

To everyone's complete surprise, Mary Anne said, "I kind of liked the way they tasted." She looked at me and her eyes widened. "Kristy? Are you turning *green*."

"She got you, Kristy," said Dawn.

Mary Anne looked sheepishly pleased. She had gotten me. After about a zillion gross food comments at lunch, which have made Mary Anne turn green, she had gotten me.

"Eeeeeeee!"

I flinched, but I didn't jump this time. I waited for someone to shout, "You're it!"

"ARRRRorow, arrowww!"

Boo-Boo?

"Shannon! No!" cried David Michael.

It sounded like war between the species had broken out beyond the kitchen door. That brought us all to our feet. We dashed into the hall and I led the way toward the noise.

Lou was standing on the couch in the den. She was holding a very angry Boo-Boo high above her head, while she bounced up and down on the sofa cushions.

Why hadn't Boo-Boo torn Lou's arms to shreds? Scratched her eyes? Because Lou had stuffed Boo-Boo in a pillowcase, and all I could see were the very tips of his claws, like needles poking out of a pin cushion the wrong way.

Shannon was leaping around below, barking excitedly while David Michael tried to pull her away by the collar. Karen was standing at the foot of the couch with her hands on her hips, her face flushed angrily. Linny, Hannie, and Andrew looked on. Thank goodness Emily was elsewhere. And thank goodness Mom or Watson or Nannie hadn't reached the den yet.

"Jump!" Lou taunted Shannon. "Jump!"

"Lou! Stop that right now!" I ordered.

"Here, Shannon. Jump." Lou swung the pillowcase invitingly and Shannon leaped up after it, toppling David Michael.

I strode to the sofa and reached for the pillowcase.

Lou looked down, then let go just before I could grasp it. The pillowcase landed on top of me and I fell back, trying to protect my face and other exposed parts from Boo-Boo's furious claws. He dug a couple of holes in my arms as he made his escape. The next thing I knew I was lying on the floor with Shannon ecstatically licking my face, major flesh wounds on my arms, and a circle of faces looking down at me.

"Are you okay, Kristy?" Karen asked worriedly.

"I'm fine," I said through gritted teeth.

I stood up and looked around the room until I found Lou. She was standing off to one side, watching me in a detached, disinterested sort of way.

"Lou McNally," I said, "don't you ever, *ever* do something like that again. It is cruel to tease animals."

Lou shrugged. "I was just playing."

"Tormenting helpless animals is not playing. Do you understand?"

Lou reached over and slapped David Michael on the shoulder. "You're it," she said, and ran out of the room.

David Michael looked at me anxiously.

"Go on," I said resignedly.

It seemed as if we had barely settled down in the kitchen again when a horrible new noise met our ears.

Crash!

Somehow I wasn't surprised to find Shannon backing in circles in the living room, pawing at her face, which was tied up in a scarf

so she couldn't see. She backed into a bookcase and knocked half a dozen books off, then
yelped when one hit her.

"What's going on?" I demanded. (Talk
about *déjà vu!*)

Hannie explained, "It's a game. We were
seeing if Shannon could find her bone blind-
folded. We hid it on the chair."

"Who did this?" I asked, reaching down to
untie the scarf. Shannon, none the worse for
the wear, gave the air a couple of experimental
sniffs, then zeroed in on her bone.

Everyone looked at Lou. What a surprise.

Lou shrugged. "I used to know a dog who
could do that."

I took a deep breath. "Even if you did, Shannon is just a puppy and she doesn't understand."

"She's not very smart," said Lou.

David Michael entered the room then, just
in time to hear Lou's words. (I'd wondered
where he was. I didn't *think* he'd let Lou do
that to Shannon.)

"She is too!" said David Michael. "Especially for a puppy."

"I wouldn't have a dumb old dog as dumb
as her," said Lou.

"That's enough," I said. With the help of
the rest of the BSC we settled everyone down
and involved the kids in quieter pursuits (we

hoped), then made our weary way back to the breakfast table.

"Silence *is* golden," said Mary Anne with a sigh as we finished breakfast at last.

"Yeah," I agreed. I looked around at everyone. "And you know what? I feel sorry for Lou. But she is the absolute worst kid I have ever met."

Not one single person disagreed with me.

CHAPTER 11

Saturday

It was my turn to sit with the Papadakises and the Worst Kid Ever. I have to admit, I hadn't been looking forward to the job, even though I was trying to think positive thoughts about it. But something in my brain kept repeating, "This is going to be the worst job ever." And five minutes after Mr. and Mrs. Papadakis left, when I found Lou pretending to flush Noodle the Poodle's favorite Day-Glo orange tennis ball down the toilet while Noodle barked and Sari watched, I was sure I was right...

"Hey there, what's going on?" Dawn tried to sound calm as she stood in the bathroom doorway.

None of the three occupants of the bathroom answered. Sari and Noodle were bent over the toilet. Noodle's tongue was lolling out and her tail was wagging. Sari's mouth was open, too.

Without looking up, Lou flushed the toilet again.

This set Noodle off and she began barking wildly. Sari clutched the edge of the toilet and looked up at Lou.

"Wheeee!" said Lou.

"Wheee!" said Sari.

"Hey!" said Dawn again. She ran to the toilet, bravely reached in, and retrieved the tennis ball.

"Hey!" exclaimed Lou. "What's the big deal?"

Drying the tennis ball off with a towel (which she threw in the hamper), Dawn answered, "The deal is, you could stop up the toilet. And even if you didn't, I don't think you should tease Noodle like that." Dawn didn't add that she hated to think what kind of ideas Sari had gotten from the display.

Lou said, "I wasn't teasing Noodle. I once knew a dog who used to like to drop her toys in the toilet. It was her favorite game."

"If you want to play Noodle's favorite game, why don't you take her into the backyard and play fetch?" Dawn held out the damp tennis ball and Noodle gave a hopeful bark.

But Lou shook her head. "Never mind," she said and walked indignantly out of the bathroom. Dawn gave the tennis ball to Noodle and took Sari's hand. "You're all wet, Sari."

"Wet," agreed Sari.

"Let's go pick out something nice and dry to wear, okay?"

Sari went peacefully along with the idea (although she insisted on wearing one blue tennis shoe and one red one to match her red, white, and blue playsuit). "Very Claudia," Dawn told Sari approvingly. Sari completed her ensemble by grabbing her latest favorite toy, a plush green pickle with yellow felt eyes and a big red felt smile. (Personally, although Dawn is a vegetarian, she felt the pickle was sort of scary.) Then they went downstairs to the Papadakises' playroom just in time to hear Lou say, "Cats are stupid. Everyone knows that."

"They are not," said Linny.

"If they're so smart, why can't they do tricks?"

"Pat the Cat knows a lot of tricks." That was Hannie.

"Oh yeah? Like what?"

"She . . . chases balls," said Hannie.

"Any cat'll do that," Lou told Hannie scornfully. "That's not a trick, that's a . . . a . . ."

"Trait," supplied Dawn, coming into the room. "It's something an animal does instinctively, so Lou is right. It's not a trick."

"Trick or trait!" cried Linny.

Dawn rolled her eyes at Linny's awful pun, but she couldn't help smiling. Then she went on, "Just because Pat doesn't do things a dog would do, doesn't mean she isn't smart. She's just a different kind of smart than, say, a dog. I knew someone in California who had cats that came when you whistled. She'd trained them to do that."

"Could we train Pat to do that?" asked Linny. "Just like Noodle?"

"I don't know. You could try. If you whistle every time you feed her, maybe after awhile, she'll connect whistling with food, and come when you whistle."

"Wow," said Linny, sounding truly impressed.

For a moment, Lou looked almost enthusiastic, too. But when Dawn gave her an encouraging smile, she turned away. So Dawn said absentmindedly, "Oh. I almost forgot. I have a carob brownie recipe I want to test.

Your mother said it was okay to try it . . . if anybody wants to . . . "

"Brownies!" said Hannie, skipping toward the kitchen.

"What's carob?" asked Linny.

"Like chocolate, only healthier."

"Yuck," said Lou. But she and Linny and Hannie followed Dawn and Sari to the kitchen, where Dawn had left her backpack with the ingredients in it. Soon Linny and Hannie and Lou were wrapped up in aprons. (Lou, however, had insisted that she didn't need one and that aprons were for sissies, until Dawn put her own apron on and gave Lou a Look and even then, Lou wouldn't tie the sash. She just tucked it into the waist of her jeans.) Sari sat in her high chair, banging her spoon on a wooden bowl.

"Dawn opened the carob chips. "Here. Want to taste some?"

Sari immediately opened her mouth, like a hungry bird. She ate her carob chips thoughtfully, then banged on the bowl some more. Dawn wasn't sure whether she was signaling approval or disapproval. Hannie liked them, though, and Linny said they were okay. Lou shrugged.

Things were going along smoothly until Dawn turned her back and Lou scooped up some batter and, instead of eating it, flapped it on top of Hannie's head. "Cowpie, cowpie, Hannie's got a cowpie on her head," sang Lou.

Hannie's mouth dropped open. (So did Dawn's.)

"Lou!" Dawn exclaimed.

Hannie burst into tears. "I hate you!" she shrieked. "I hate you!"

Lou leaned over and stared into Hannie's swimming eyes. "And I hate you," she said.

And that was when Dawn did something completely uncharacteristic: She grabbed Lou, lifted her clear up off the floor, and carried her out of the kitchen. "Put me down!" commanded Lou.

Dawn kept going without answering. When she reached Lou's room, she carried her in and dropped her on the bed.

"Congratulations, Lou," said Dawn through gritted teeth. "You get to stay in your room until you can behave. I wonder how long *that* will be."

Lou gave Dawn a measured look, then said, "I hate you, too."

Dawn turned her head and returned to the kitchen.

It took a little while for Dawn to restore order. She washed the batter out of Hannie's hair, and put the brownies in the oven, promising samples for Hannie and Linny after they'd finished some of their homework. "I have a book to read," said Hannie. "For a real book report. Can I read it to Sari?"

"Sure you can," said Dawn.

"Come on, Sari," said Hannie in a very grown-up voice, her tears forgotten. Soon Hannie and Sari were sitting together on the couch in the den.

Linny went upstairs to his room to begin his homework. At last the house was quiet.

Collapsing at the kitchen table, Dawn began to twist one end of her long, pale blonde hair around and around her finger. She was trying to enjoy the smell of carob brownies baking, and the sound of silence. But she couldn't. For some reason, it felt too quiet.

So she did what every good baby-sitter does when things are too quiet. She decided to find out what was wrong. She started by checking on the kids.

Hannie and Sari were doing fine in the den. Linny was so absorbed in his homework that he didn't even notice when she peeked around his door.

But Lou was not in her room.

Dawn was tempted to panic. In fact, her first thought was, Oh no, Lou's run away and it's all my fault. But she took a deep breath and decided to check out the rest of the house first.

She found Lou in Hannie's room, sitting on the floor. Her back was to the door as Dawn pushed it open. Her thin shoulders were hunched over.

"Lou?" said Dawn softly.

"Go away," said Lou fiercely. She half turned and Dawn saw that she was cradling one of Hannie's dolls in her arms. And she'd been crying.

Dawn's first impulse was to put her arms around Lou and cradle her the way Lou was cradling that doll. But her instincts made her sit down quietly next to Lou instead. She didn't mention the doll or the fact that Lou had been crying. She just said, "Oh, Lou."

Lou hunched forward again. "I hate you," she whispered. "I hate everybody."

Then she started to cry again.

She cried as angrily and intensely as she had done everything else since she'd come to live with the Papadakises. But along with the flood of tears came a flood of words.

"He left me. I want my father. He left me!"

"Oh, Lou," said Dawn again. "He wouldn't have if he could have helped it. You know he loved you very, very much."

"And Jay's gone and my mother doesn't want me. *She* left. She didn't have to leave."

"Maybe she did. You don't know what happened."

"I want my mother. I want my *mother*. I

want to go home . . . " Lou clutched the doll convulsively and began to cry even harder.

"Shhh," whispered Dawn. "It's okay, Lou. It'll be okay. You have friends here. We'll take care of you. And things will work out."

Lou shook her head, but gradually her crying became less anguished. "I want my mother," she whispered very, very softly.

Dawn leaned over and tried to put her arm around Lou. Lou jerked back like she'd been burned.

"Don't do that," she cried. "You can't do that to me."

"Lou, what's the matter?" asked Dawn, pulling back.

"Don't *touch* me," Lou gasped. "You'll just be nice to me and pretend you like me and then you'll leave me. That's what everyone always does. Even m-my doggg . . . "

Lou almost started crying again, but she dug her fist in her eyes and kept herself from it.

"You had a dog?" asked Dawn.

"He was a *good* dog. He was smart. His name was Jingles." For a moment Lou's face brightened. "He knew all kinds of tricks and everything. He understood what you said to him." Then her face closed up again. "But he left.He got out and ran away and never came back. And then our father . . . " She took a deep breath and almost shouted ". . . died."

Oh, thought Dawn. That's why Lou was pestering all the animals. Keeping them — and us — all from getting too close to her. Testing us.

Aloud she said, "It's not always like that, Lou."

Lou didn't answer, so Dawn went on. "And even if someone is gone, you remember him. Your father loved you. He didn't stop loving you. And you didn't stop loving him. You'll always remember him and love him. That's okay. That's how it's supposed to be."

Lou still didn't answer. Dawn cautiously patted Lou's shoulder. She flinched, but she didn't pull away.

Standing up, Dawn said, "I smell some carob brownies that are just about ready. Why don't you come down and have some with us in a little while?"

Shortly afterward, as Dawn was cutting the brownies and handing them around to Linny, Hannie, and Sari, Lou came into the kitchen. She didn't look at Dawn as she took her brownie and sat down at the table.

"These aren't bad," said Linny, watching Lou out of the corner of his eye.

"I think they taste good," declared Hannie. She snuck a quick look at Lou, then looked away.

"I'm sorry," Lou said to Hannie, not quite looking at her.

There was a little silence. Then Hannie said, "Okay."

Lou took a bite of her brownie and made a face. "I like chocolate better," she said.

That evening back at her house, Dawn called me and told me about the afternoon's events. "She's not the worst kid ever, Kristy," Dawn told me. "She's the saddest."

CHAPTER 12

The woman on the phone said her name was Mrs. Graves and that she was Lou McNally's social worker. She had a pleasant voice.

"I'm Kristy Thomas," I told her. "I'm baby-sitting for the Papadakises. They're out right now and won't be home for another hour. May I take a message?"

"Well," said Mrs. Graves, "this is important. I need to talk to Lou as soon as possible. Would you tell the Papadakises, if they should call, that I'm on my way over? Or I'll see them when I get there."

She hung up.

I stared at the phone for a moment, worrying. Then I pulled out the piece of paper with the list of all the places Mrs. Papadakis could be reached. She had called me at home at the last minute to sit for an hour while she took Pat the Cat to the vet for her yearly shots (the veterinarian had had a cancellation).

But Mrs. Papadakis had just left. Plus, I knew she planned to stop at the cleaners on the way home, but I didn't know which one.

What if Mrs. Graves arrived before Mrs. Papadakis came home?

I decided I'd better tell Lou that Mrs. Graves was on her way.

I don't know what I expected, exactly. Lou had seemed a little subdued when I'd gotten there, for which I was grateful. In fact, things had been unusually calm.

She wasn't subdued now. When I gave her the message her face lit up and she actually smiled at me — and I suddenly realized what a cute kid she was. What she said surprised me even more than the smile. "She found my mother. My mother's coming to get me!"

"Ah, Lou," I said, "she didn't tell me anything like that. She just said it was important."

But Lou didn't hear me. She whirled away and began spinning around, almost ricocheting from room to room.

By the time Mrs. Graves arrived, she was in a fever of anticipation.

"Why don't you go in the living room?" I suggested.

Mrs. Graves smiled, a smile as pleasant as her voice sounded over the phone. "Thank you, Kristy," she said. "Come on, Lou. We have some important news to discuss."

"I *know*," said Lou, smiling that big, new, wonderful kid smile.

I turned away from the door with a sinking heart. I wasn't trying to eavesdrop, but I heard Mrs. Graves say, "You and Jay have a new home. And it is with a family."

Could Lou have been right? Had they found her mother?

"Your father's brother and his wife — your aunt and uncle — were so excited to hear about you two. You'll be leaving here in less than a week for your new home!"

Mrs. Graves sounded so excited for Lou! Did she expect Lou to be excited, too?

Probably. But Lou was enraged. "*Noooooooo!*" she screamed at the top of her lungs. "*No, no, no, no, no, no, no!*"

"Lou!" exclaimed Mrs. Graves.

"Where is my *mother*? I want my mother!"

"Lou," said Mrs. Graves. Then, "Kristy?"

I hurried into the living room to find Lou pushing over stools and chairs, and grabbing pillows off the sofa and hurling them around. Mrs. Graves tried to catch Lou but she slid away, falling over a chair.

"No," she kept screaming. "No, no, no!"

"Lou?" We hadn't even heard Mrs. Papadakis come in. Lou snatched up a pillow and threw it with all her might.

"What happened?" asked Mrs. Papadakis.

"I told her we'd found her aunt and uncle. That she and Jay were to live with them . . ."

"NO!" screamed Lou. A pillow crashed into the wall and a picture slid down and fell over. Mrs. Papadakis reached for Lou but she evaded her to run into the dining room and around the table.

Crash! A row of pictures on the sideboard were swept to the floor.

"Lou," I called.

"It's okay, Kristy," said Mrs. Papadakis. "I'll take it from here."

"All right," I said hastily and backed out of the room.

As I left the adults to try to catch Lou and calm her down, I could hear her still: "I won't, I won't. You can't make me."

At home that afternoon, I had a hard time concentrating. I kept hearing Lou's voice: "Where is my mother?" And I kept remembering what Dawn had said: "Kristy, she's not the worst kid ever. She's the saddest kid ever."

Then just before dinner the doorbell rang. "Kristy!" my mom called.

I ran downstairs to find my mother and Mrs. Papadakis standing in the hall. Mrs. Papadakis's warm brown eyes were dark with worry. "Oh, Kristy," she said. "Have you seen Lou? She went on such a rampage . . . I took her to her room and she ripped it apart and then she just ran out before I could stop her."

At that moment David Michael came tearing in through the kitchen from the backyard. "Have you seen it?" he demanded. "Have you seen Karen's playhouse?"

"Oh, no," I said with a sudden premonition.

"It's *wrecked*," said David Michael. "Totalled but good."

My eyes met Mrs. Papadakis's. *Lou.*

"We'll find her," I said with more confidence than I felt.

"Yes, we can all help," my mother told Mrs. Papadakis. "We'll find her. She can't have gone far."

Within a few minutes, Mom, Watson (holding Emily Michelle), Charlie, Sam, Nannie, and everyone else in the neighborhood, it seemed, were out looking for Lou.

I walked slowly down the street, calling Lou's name and trying to think. Where would she go? Would she really run far away? Would she try to go to the bus station, maybe, and catch a bus? But she didn't have any money. At least, I didn't think she did. And besides, they wouldn't let an eight-year-old girl get on the bus alone without asking some questions. Would they?

I realized I was staring at a swing set in someone's backyard. And then I suddenly remembered Lou telling me about the stream in the park near her old house. I thought of the brook near the playground. Maybe Lou had gone there.

By then it was almost dark, and at first I thought I had been wrong. But soon I noticed a movement at the bottom of the bank. "Lou?" I pushed aside some branches and saw her, sitting on a rock near the trickle of water.

"Lou," I said again, and scrambled down to join her. "Everyone's looking for you, Lou."

"Yeah," she said tonelessly.

"It's time to go home." (Home? Me and my big mouth.)

"I don't have a home," replied Lou. She looked at me. It was hard to see her expression in the gathering dusk, but the flatness slid out of her voice, to be replaced by such sadness it made me hurt. "I don't have a home or a family. What happened to my mother?"

"I don't know, Lou."

"She's gone. Just like everyone else. No one ever stays. No one."

"You have an aunt and uncle who want you to be their family."

"It's not the same."

"No," I said. "But you can still be a family."

Lou didn't answer. After a minute she stood up. She shrugged. "Let's go," she said.

CHAPTER 13

"It's time, Kristy!"

"I'll be right there," I told Karen. I pulled on my sweater and trotted downstairs. Then all of us — Mom, Watson, Nannie, Andrew, David Michael, Charlie, Sam, Emily Michelle, Karen, and me — went across the street to the Papadakises'.

It was Saturday afternoon, but I wasn't going to a baby-sitting job. I was going to a party, a celebration for Lou McNally and her new family. It was a send-off as well. The whole neighborhood was invited, plus the members of the BSC.

We could hear the mumble-mumble-laugh of party noise before Mr. Papadakis opened the door. Our family split up almost immediately and was absorbed into the noise and high spirits. I stood for a moment getting my bearings until I saw Mary Anne and Logan by the refreshment table. But before I could head in their direction, Dawn threaded her way through the stream of people.

"Kristy," she called.

"Hi," I said. "Where's everybody else?"

Of course I meant Stacey and Claudia and Jessi and Mallory. And of course, Dawn knew what I meant. "They'll be here," she said. "Listen, Mrs. Papadakis told me Lou hasn't come downstairs yet. You want to go see what's keeping her?"

"Okay," I said.

"She's probably a little nervous about meeting her aunt and uncle," suggested Dawn as we climbed the stairs.

"They came over to the Papadakises' last night for a little while," I told Dawn. "So they're not complete strangers."

Dawn nodded seriously. "That's good," she said.

With a sinking feeling, I saw that Lou's door was closed. Had she locked herself in her room? Was she going to refuse to come out? What if she'd run away again?

"Oh no," I said, my voice rising.

Dawn gave me a puzzled look, and knocked on the door.

Lou's voice said, "Who is it?"

I felt pretty foolish, but at least Dawn didn't ask me what was going on.

"It's Dawn and Kristy," she said. "May we come in?"

A moment later the door opened and Lou stepped back to let us by. She was wearing the same outfit she'd been wearing the day she arrived at the Papadakises.' Over her shoulder on the bed I could see a suitcase, her backpack, and a plaid skirt and a matching sweater. I had a feeling she was supposed to be changing into that skirt and sweater.

"Looks like you're all packed and ready," said Dawn.

"Yeah," replied Lou.

"Nice sweater," added Dawn. "Good color for you."

Lou scowled.

I had a sudden flash of intuition. "You know what, Lou? I don't like to wear skirts. In fact," I said, motioning to what I was wearing (my best jeans, a turtleneck, a sweater, and sneakers), "this is pretty much all I like to wear. But I like a new sweater sometimes."

"Maybe," said Lou, looking more thoughtful now than scowly.

"Lou!" called Mrs. Papadakis.

"We'll meet you downstairs," Dawn said.

A few minutes later Lou came into the rec room, where everyone had gathered. She was wearing her new sweater — over her old overalls. Dawn had been right. The color did look good on her. Or maybe it was the way her face lit up when Mrs. Graves and Jay walked into the room.

"Jay!" shrieked Lou. She hurled herself across the room.

And Jay, although he was eleven and a boy, gave her a big hug — before letting go and punching her on the arm. She danced away and then back, and punched him. "Jay, Jay, Jay," she said.

He grinned. He and Lou looked a lot alike. They were both wiry and strong. But Jay had freckles and didn't seem so suspicious. Just reserved.

"Want some punch?" asked Lou and punched him in the arm again giggling. I looked up and my eyes met Mary Anne's. This was a Lou we hadn't seen before.

A few minutes later the McNallys arrived. Mrs. McNally was a tall, calm-looking woman with laugh lines at the corners of her eyes. Mr. McNally was a little shorter, and more brisk, with a kind face. They seemed to know just how to act with Lou and Jay. When Jay offered each of them his hand to shake, they took it solemnly. And when Lou imitated Jay and offered them her hand, they shook hands with her, too. Then Mr. McNally cleared his throat and said, "Lou, we have something we think you'd like."

For a moment the old Lou was back. She folded her arms and looked wary. Mr. McNally cleared his throat again and went on as if he hadn't noticed. "Jay suggested it, as a matter of fact."

Lou unfolded her arms and looked almost curious as Jay broke into a broad grin. Mrs. McNally caught his eye, winked, and nodded toward the door.

"All *right*," said Jay. He punched the air with his fist. "Wait here, Lou!" He raced out of the room. A moment later the door opened and a fat, black Labrador puppy came tumbling in with Jay behind him.

The puppy stood for a moment looking around, her tail wagging so hard her whole body wiggled.

Lou's mouth dropped open — and I admit, I held my breath. What would Lou do?

Lou looked at Jay and at the puppy and then at the McNallys. At last she found her voice.

"For me?" she whispered.

"She's all yours," said Jay excitedly. "She came from the shelter. She's three months old, and she's getting a new home the same time we are."

I don't even know if Lou heard what Jay said. She sank to her knees, held out her hands, and said in a crooning voice I'd never heard her use, "Here, puppy. Here, girl."

Seeing someone down on her level, the puppy leaped forward with an excited yip. In another minute she and Lou were tangled up together, oblivious to the rest of the world.

I felt an unexpected lump in my throat. Fortunately, Claudia's voice said in my ear, "Look. M&M chocolate chip cookies. Boy, Mrs. Papadakis knows how to give a party!" and I ended up swallowing hard — and laughing instead.

I looked around at the streamers and the long table filled with all kinds of goodies — grown-up goodies like tuna dip (yeccch) and the really good stuff, like M&M chocolate chip cookies and double cheese popcorn. There was a big sign above the table that said *Hurray for Lou McNally*.

David Michael and Linny had approached Jay and were now talking to him. I deduced by their gestures that it was sports talk. I half expected to see Lou with them, but when I spotted her again she was kneeling on the floor, one sock on, the other in her hand, trailing it along the ground for the puppy. The Three Musketeers were standing next to her.

Just then the puppy squatted and made a puddle on the floor.

"Uh-oh," said Nancy.

"It's okay," said Hannie. "I'll get some paper towels."

Lou nodded. She showed the puppy the puddle and said firmly, "No. No." Then she picked the puppy up (who immediately tried to lick her face). She stood there for a moment, looking around the room. Her eyes met Mr. McNally's. "I'm taking my puppy outside for a minute, so she knows where to go," Lou said.

He smiled and nodded.

"Me, too," said Karen to the room in general.

Watching them go, I said to Mary Anne, "Is *that* Lou McNally?"

"Try calling her Louisa and see!" suggested Mary Anne.

A few minutes later, when they returned, Hannie helped Lou clean up the puddle and the four girls sat down in a circle around the puppy.

"She is gigundoly cute," said Karen.

"You are soooo lucky," Nancy added.

Lou looked up briefly, then down at the puppy.

"What are you going to name her?" asked Hannie.

"Something good," said Lou. "I haven't decided yet." She reached out and rolled the sock into a ball. Then she scooted it across the circle to Karen. The puppy pounced — and missed completely.

Laughing, Karen rolled the sock back to Lou. Soon the girls were rolling the sock back and forth, and the puppy was spinning in ecstatic circles.

At last she caught it (Karen rolled it straight to her and it bumped her on the nose). Head held high, she walked over to Lou and collapsed, puppy-fashion, into instant sleep, the sock still in her mouth. Lou cradled the puppy in her arms, then looked up at the Three Musketeers.

"I'm sorry I wrecked your old playhouse," she said.

Karen said, "It was a *new* playhouse . . . but it's okay."

Hannie and Nancy nodded. Then Karen said, "We were going to change it to a clubhouse, anyway. But now we're going to do something different."

"Yeah," said Hannie. "We need to build something new."

"A fort?" suggested Lou.

Hannie hesitated and Nancy jumped in. "I know. A castle!"

"With a moat," Lou said.

Karen's eyes grew round with excitement. "A moat. With . . . with bewitched goldfish in it."

Lou looked startled. Pleased with the success of this, Karen lowered her voice and said eerily, "Next door to me lives a scary, scary witch. Her name is Morbidda Destiny . . ."

I turned to find Mrs. Papadakis and the McNallys next to me. "This is Kristy," Mrs. Papadakis said to them. "She's an excellent baby-sitter . . . in fact, she's done some baby-sitting for us while Lou has been here."

"Hello," I said, as Mrs. Papadakis began to thread her way back across the rec room.

"I hear you found Lou the other day. Smart thinking," said Mrs. McNally.

I felt myself blushing. "Thank you. I think getting her the puppy was a great idea."

"It was Jay's idea," said Mr. McNally.

"Lou's had a hard time," Mrs. McNally added. "So has Jay. It's going to be different now, though. For all of us." She looked so pleased and excited, and well, comfortable, that I believed it was true.

"Time to cut the new family cake!" announced Mr. Papadakis. "Would the McNally family please come forward?"

As Mr. and Mrs. McNally, and Jay and Lou (and the puppy) went to the table at the front of the room, I realized that the BSC had gathered around me. It seemed fitting. Lou was one sitting charge we'd never forget.

So we stood together, applauding the

speeches and the cutting of the cake. And we laughed at the two going-away gifts the Papadakises gave Lou.

She unwrapped one and held it up by a leg: It was a baby doll. With an expert gesture she cradled it in her arm next to the puppy (who nuzzled it sleepily).

The other gift was a football.

"Awwright," said Jay.

"Thank you," said Lou. She looked over at Jay. "Would you like to hold my present?" she asked him.

"You bet," replied Jay.

Everyone laughed when Lou handed him the doll.

CHAPTER 14

The party was winding down. We'd eaten and drunk almost everything, and people were beginning to drift away. An informal sort of receiving line (or maybe I mean departing line) had formed at the door, where Mr. and Mrs. Papadakis and Jay and Mr. and Mrs. McNally were shaking hands and talking to people as they left.

Lou and the Three Musketeers were nowhere in sight.

"I can't believe it," said Dawn. "I have a feeling things are going to be a lot easier for Lou from now on."

"And maybe a little harder for the McNallys," I couldn't resist adding. Mary Anne gave me a surprised look and I added, "Listen, the McNallys just went from being a no-kid family to a two-kid family. They're bound to run into a few problems."

"You know what I think?" asked Claudia.

"I think Lou is going to always be getting into some kind of trouble. Not *bad* trouble — but she's very creative, from what I've seen and heard about her and . . . "

" . . . and creative people get in lots of trouble, Claud?" teased Stacey.

"Creative people think differently. Sometimes that can get you into trouble," said Claudia loftily.

"It sure makes life more interesting, though," said Mallory. "I mean, don't you just hate baby-sitting for perfect children?"

Pow pow pow!

We all jumped about a mile at the noise, then looked around to see Lou grinning hugely with delight. She and the Three Musketeers had pulled the balloons down and were kicking and chasing them around the room, with the puppy bouncing enthusiastically at Lou's side. She pounced on a balloon while we watched, gave it a good shake, and . . .

POW!

"Creative, huh?" muttered Jessi. "I'll let you know how I feel about boring perfect children when I meet any boring perfect children."

I felt myself tense up. What would the McNallys do about the noise and confusion Lou was creating just now? I half turned, wanting to protect Lou somehow.

But Mrs. McNally started to laugh. "Lou, take those balloons outside — if it's all right with the Papadakises — and finish them off there."

Mrs. Papadakis nodded, and Lou, Hannie, Nancy, and Karen began to scoop up armfuls of balloons. The puppy, leaping joyously, was no help at all.

"Be careful your dog doesn't swallow any balloon pieces," Mr. McNally added as they trooped past him. He gave Lou's shoulder a quick affectionate pat.

She looked up and nodded solemnly.

A minute later, the sound of balloons continuing to pop came like firecrackers through the open door.

Meanwhile the members of the BSC got in line and filed out, handshake over handshake, into the yard to watch the last of the balloons bursting while the Papadakises and the McNallys put Lou's stuff in the car. She had one more suitcase now than when she had arrived.

I reached into my jacket pocket and felt the corner of the package I'd been carrying all afternoon. I walked to the car as Mr. McNally swung Lou's suitcase into the trunk. "Here," I said. "This is for Lou. For later on." I handed him the package. "It's a book," I said, as if he couldn't tell by the shape and size.

"That's a nice thought, Kristy," he said. "I know she'll appreciate it."

I shrugged, thought of Lou, and couldn't help but smile. Maybe, I thought. "I hope so," I said aloud.

Mrs. McNally waved. "Lou! Time to go."

For a moment longer the four girls raced around in the late afternoon light, chasing the last balloon. Then Karen jumped on it and they all screamed as it exploded with a satisfying final pop.

"Okay, I'm coming," said Lou. "Come on, girl. Come on." She patted her leg and the puppy ambled over to her, panting. "*Good* girl. You are so smart."

She gathered the puppy in her arms, and turned to face the Three Musketeers.

"Good-bye," said Lou.

"Good-bye," said Karen.

" 'Bye," echoed Hannie and Nancy.

"Good luck with your castle," added Lou.

"You, too," said Hannie. "I mean, good luck with your new house and everything."

"Yeah." Lou looked around with a little frown, as if she were trying to remember something. Then she said again, "Good-bye," and turned and ran to the car. She didn't scramble up the hood this time, but holding the puppy carefully, climbed in the back seat next to Jay.

150

A minute later, the car had backed out of the driveway and was pulling away.

We waved and waved until it was out of sight.

As the car disappeared, Mrs. Graves, who was standing next to me, said softly, "Lou is lucky. The stories of most foster children do not have such happy endings."

I nodded. But I wasn't sure it was such a happy ending. Lou had lost her father and her home, and she would probably never know the mother she longed for. Still . . .

Maybe the book I'd given her would help. I wondered what Lou would think of *The Great Gilly Hopkins*. After all, it was a story about a kid kind of like her.

I said good-bye to everyone, and headed across the street for home.

I almost didn't check the mailbox. I'd almost given up. In fact, I'd been at home for twenty minutes before I remembered to check it. And even when I reached inside and pulled out a small, flat package addressed to me and saw a Hollywood agent's return address, I didn't believe it.

But it was true. As I walked back across the lawn and unwrapped the package (a dangerous thing to do — I was so excited I almost walked into a tree) I realized we had at least one super donation for the auction. Lorne

151

Conners, whose album had won four Grammies the year before, had sent us an amazing T-shirt — with her autograph scrawled across the front.

I could hardly wait to call my friends and tell them the news. I was sure this was just the beginning.

And I was right. During the next few days, all kinds of things arrived from all kinds of people, complete with celebrity letters: Jessi received old toe shoes and a note from a famous prima ballerina; one of Mallory's favorite authors sent a boxed set of her books, each one autographed; Stacey took a package notice into the post office and came back, in a daze, with a piece of registered mail — a baseball autographed with the names of the entire baseball team that had just won the pennant; Mallory received a second package. It contained the warm-up blanket belonging to the horse that had most recently won the Kentucky Derby, and a note from the horse's trainer. But best of all was what Cam Geary sent Mary Anne.

I had to hold the phone away from my ear when she called me about it. "Cam!" she screamed. "Cam! Cam! Cam!"

"No, it's me. Kristy."

"Kristy! Cam!"

"You heard from Cam Geary?" I asked.

"Yes. And you'll never guess what he sent!"

"I give up," I said.

"The actual jacket that he wore in his movie!"

I screamed too, then. "Cam Geary! I don't believe it!"

"I'm wearing it right now. Cam Geary's actual jacket that has actually touched him . . ."

The auction was going to be a success.

We had another success to celebrate, too.

A couple of days before Lou had left, my friends and I had mailed cards to her at her new address, so she'd have something waiting for her when she arrived. Now she'd written us back. The first letters said pretty much the same thing: "Thank you for your card. I liked it very much. How are you doing? I am okay. It is okay here."

But then I received another letter from Lou:

Dear Kristy,
 Thank you for my book. I have never had a book of mine to keep before. Here in my new house I have a bookcase. It is in my own room. I am painting my room any color I want. I am painting it red. Uncle Mac is putting stars on the ceiling. You can see them at night after the lights are turned off.

I like my book. It is a sad ending. But it is okay, anyway.

My dog sleeps on the end of my bed. She is always happy so that is what I named her — Happy. Silly dog.

Good-bye for now.

Lou

I wouldn't trade that letter for all the celebrity letters in the world.

CHAPTER 15

I saw a television movie once where the heroine (in disguise) followed a murder suspect to an auction. It was in a huge, Victorian-looking old room filled with people in big hats and dark suits, and every time anyone, so much as twitched, the auctioneer said, "Thirty, thirty, who'll make it thirty-five (twitch), thirty-five, do I hear forty?" He meant forty *thousand* dollars, not forty dollars, and of course the heroine sneezed, and ended up buying something enormously expensive.

Stacey said her parents took her with them to an auction at an art gallery in the East Village in New York once and it was sort of the same, except the people were dressed more like Claudia, including the auctioneer, who had seven pierced earrings, all diamonds, in one ear.

So I wasn't quite sure what to expect at the SMS auction. One thing I did know: Even though this was for a good cause and even though it wasn't a competition, we'd beat the socks off Cokie and her friends. Mary Anne and Logan had seen the evidence first hand.

Mary Anne had gone to the auction room at school with the Cam Geary jacket and letter. (The letter was to verify the jacket's provenance. That means proving where it came from and that it really is genuine.) Logan had wandered over to check out an enormous aquarium built into an old television, made so that when fish were in it, they looked as if they were on a television program. Mary Anne was just folding up the receipt Ms. Garcia had given to her while she searched for Mary Anne's other donation (we were replacing our ordinary donations with the celebrity items). Suddenly a certain well-known nasty voice said, "Oh, how sweet! You're donating your old clothes. Isn't that cute, Grace?"

Cokie and Grace were hovering in the doorway.

"Not exactly," said Mary Anne. Ms. Garcia handed Mary Anne her original donation and smiled. "Such a wonderful donation," she said.

Cokie interrupted. "It was easy. It's all in who you know. And of course, you need to be creative . . . "

"Yes, dear, and that's exactly what Mary

Anne and her friends have done."

Logan wandered back to Mary Anne as Ms. Garcia went on, "Creative *and* resourceful. These celebrity donations will be the hit of the auction."

As Grace's mouth dropped open and Cokie began to turn red *and* purple (and somewhere inside probably green with envy), Mary Anne said, "It's Cam Geary's old clothes, Cokie. You see, he donated this jacket — from his movie — for our auction."

Logan couldn't resist adding, as he and Mary Anne left, "It's all in who you know, right, Cokie?"

The auction was held on Friday night at the SMS auditorium and we all got dressed-up for it. I put on my best jeans and favorite sweater, and if we didn't look like we were ready for the auction in the movie, we looked pretty good. We sat together near the back of the room. I looked down the row and felt pretty proud of the BSC. And I felt even more proud as I looked at the program with the list of donations. There were a lot of great donations — including Cokie's — but ours, listed last, like the grand finale of the auction, were definitely special.

A hush fell over the auditorium and I looked up.

The SMS student council had asked a

professional auctioneer to run the program, and she'd agreed to donate her time. As the principal and the president of the student council walked onto the stage, I realized that the tiny, dark-haired woman with them had to be the auctioneer. She didn't look like the auctioneer in the movie (he'd been dressed in a tuxedo) or the one Stacey had seen in the East Village in New York. This auctioneer was wearing diamond earrings, but just one in each earlobe, and a beige suit, a silky ivory wrap blouse, pale beige stockings, and dark brown pumps. She looked like a principal or a lawyer.

The principal made a speech of welcome. Then the student council president explained the purpose of the auction and introduced the auctioneer, whose name was Ms. Thames. She explained the rules of the auction: things would be brought on stage in groups as listed in the program. After every item in each group was sold, the group of items would be transported to the lunchroom behind the auditorium where buyers could pay for them and pick them up. I was relieved to hear that you had to raise your hand to signal a bid.

Ms. Thames lifted her gavel.

Another expectant hush fell over the auditorium.

Then the gavel fell and the auction began.

The auctioneer talked fast (just like in the movies) but not so fast you couldn't understand her. It was pretty amazing to listen to her, especially when she actually did (without taking a breath) say things like, "Going once, going twice, SOLD! The oak breakfront with the beveled glass is sold to the gentleman in the pinstripe suit."

I thought Mom and Watson would probably buy an antique. Still, I was surprised when the auctioneer said, "Going once, going twice, SOLD! The hand crank phonograph and collection of Cole Porter seventy-eight records . . ." and realized Mom and Watson had bought that.

"Guess they're not going to bid on the trip to Power Records," teased Claudia.

"Oh, brother," I said.

A little while later, I saw a hand shoot up into the air, followed by someone jumping up and down. The arm waved frantically and a little ripple of laughter spread out in the crowd.

When the auctioneer said, "Sold!" a familiar voice cried out, "Gigundoly super!" and another familiar voice said, "Indoor voice, Karen."

So I guess Karen's goldfish would be getting a new home — the TV aquarium.

Then we had another surprise: Logan bid

on a pair of pearl earrings donated by Klein Jewelers. When the auctioneer said, "Sold!" we all turned to look at Logan — except Mary Anne. She was staring down at her hands, blushing.

Logan looked back at us. "You never know when you can use a pair of earrings," he drawled. Then he reached out and held one of Mary Anne's hands and even though her head was still bent and she was still blushing, I could see she was smiling, too.

Guess who bought the three-minute shopping spree at Power Records?

Cokie's father. He bid a huge amount of money right off the bat (in a bored sort of voice) and then no one else would bid.

"So much for that," muttered Stacey. "What a flop."

And it was, too. No one *oohed* or *aahed* or anything.

But then, I bid on something *I* had donated. When the celebrity items came up, I bid on an autographed photograph of J.C. Kalisi, one of the first women ever to win an Olympic Gold Medal in track. She went on to be one of the first women coaches. She's retired now, but she does feature commentary on television sometimes for sports events.

She's kind of a heroine of mine. I actually didn't expect many people to bid on the photograph — but I ended up spending several hours worth of baby-sitting savings!

The rest of the celebrity items sold for a bit more. In fact, a lot more. The sight of Cam Geary's jacket made the auditorium break into excited murmurings, and the bidding became pretty intense. When it reached a hundred dollars, I almost fell off my chair.

The girl who bought it (I think she was a high school senior) jumped up victoriously when Ms. Thames banged the gavel down and said, "Sold!"

The celebrity items were definitely the hit of the auction. And we all jumped up to cheer when, a few minutes after the end of the auction, the official tabulation was announced. SMS had reached its goal for the new computers.

"We did it!" cried Mary Anne, hugging me and Logan and everyone else within reach.

Cheers and applause and bursts of laughter filled the auditorium as the crowd dispersed to pick up purchases. "I better go get my genuine autographed photograph," I said.

"Why don't we go with you," suggested Jessi.

Stacey, who hadn't stood up and was making notes on the program, said, "Wait a minute."

"What is it?" asked Claudia.

Stacey made one more note on her program, clicked her pen, and put it away. Then she looked up and grinned.

"I'm pleased to announce," she paused, then held up the program and pointed, "that the Baby-sitters Club contributed the highest ticket item of the auction."

We crowded around Stacey and leaned over to see what she was pointing at.

Item: Twenty-four (24) hours of baby-sitting to be scheduled at the convenience of the purchaser, donated by the Baby-sitters Club of Stoneybrook.

"We're pretty valuable items," said Mallory.

"We're worth more than Cam Geary's jacket," said Jessi in an awed tone of voice.

"You know what?" I said. "In the future, we really should have a little more faith in ourselves."

"Hurray for the BSC of SMS!" cried Claudia.

"Claudia," said Stacey. "You're learning how to spell!"

Laughing, we headed for the lunchroom.

About the Author

ANN M. MARTIN did *a lot* of baby-sitting when she was growing up in Princeton, New Jersey. She is a former editor of books for children, and was graduated from Smith College.

Ms. Martin lives in New York City with her cats, Mouse and Rosie. She likes ice cream and *I Love Lucy*; and she hates to cook.

Ann Martin's Apple Paperbacks include *Yours Turly, Shirley; Ten Kids, No Pets; With You and Without You; Bummer Summer;* and all the other books in the Baby-sitters Club series.

Look for #63

CLAUDIA'S F~~RIEN~~D FRIEND

"Listen Shea," I said impulsively. "Would you help me with my spelling?"

"You mean *I* get to be the teacher?"

"Yes." I handed him a magazine. "Pick some words out and help me learn to spell them."

Shea looked at the magazine I'd chosen. *Seventeen.* "How about *Sports Illustrated,* instead?" he suggested.

"You can choose your magazines, I get to choose mine," I declared.

"Oh, all right," said Shea, grinning. He opened the magazine. "Peach," he said.

"Peach?" I repeated.

"It's the color of a nail polish," explained Shea.

"Oh," I said. "P . . ." I looked at Shea. I thought about using two "e"s. I remembered Shea's rule. "E-a."

164

I stopped. Shea nodded.

"T-c-h," I muttered. No. That didn't sound right.

"Think of other words that sound like it," suggested Shea.

"Reach," I said. "Teach."

"Beach," said Shea.

"Beach? I know how to spell beach," I said.

"Peach?" asked Shea.

"The same!" I said triumphantly. "P-e-a-c-h."

"Yes!" Shea dropped the magazine and pumped both fists in the air like I'd just hit a home run.

After that I hardly noticed the rain, or the relative p-e-a-c-e coming from Jackie and Archie's end of the house. And by the time they'd come back to the den to make some more snack suggestions (it really was snack-time by now) I'd started feeling a little better about my creative spelling abilities. Shea had been a *huge* help.

When Mrs. Rodowsky got home, Shea had finished his homework. We met her in the front hall, the same as before, but the vibes between Shea and me were a good bit better.

In fact, they were great.

**Read all the books
in the Baby-sitters Club series
by Ann M. Martin**

#56 *Keep out, Claudia!*
Who wouldn't want Claudia for a baby-sitter?

#57 *Dawn Saves the Planet*
Dawn's trying to do a good thing — but she's driv-
ing everyone crazy!

#58 *Stacey's Choice*
Stacey's parents are both depending on her. But
how can she choose between them . . . again?

#59 *Mallory Hates Boys (and Gym)*
Boys and gym. What a disgusting combination!

#60 *Mary Anne's Makeover*
Everyone loves the new Mary Anne — *except* the
BSC!

#61 *Jessi and the Awful Secret*
Only Jessi knows what's really wrong with one of
the girls in her dance class.

#62 *Kristy and the Worst Kid Ever*
Need a baby-sitter for Lou? Don't call the Baby-
sitters Club!

#63 *Claudia's ~~Freind~~ Friend*
  Claudia and Shea can't spell — but they can be friends!

Super Specials:
7 *Snowbound*
  Stoneybrook gets hit by a major blizzard. Will the Baby-sitters be okay?

8 *Baby-sitters at Shadow Lake*
  Campfires, cute guys, *and* a mystery — the Baby-sitters are in for a week of summer fun!

9 *Starring the Baby-sitters Club!*
  The Baby-sitters get involved onstage and off in the SMS school production of *Peter Pan!*

Mysteries:
5 *Mary Anne and the Secret in the Attic*
  Mary Anne discovers a secret about her past and now she's afraid of the future.

6 *The Mystery at Claudia's House*
  Claudia's room has been ransacked! Can the baby-sitters track down whodunnit?

7 *Dawn and the Disappearing Dogs*
  Someone's been stealing dogs all over Stoneybrook!

8 *Jessi and the Jewel Thieves*
  Jessi and her friend Quint are busy tailing two jewel thieves all over the big apple!

Special Edition (Reader's Request):
  Logan's Story
  Being a boy baby-sitter isn't easy!

THE BABY-SITTERS CLUB®

by Ann M. Martin

❑ MG43388-1	#1	Kristy's Great Idea	$3.25
❑ MG43387-3	#10	Logan Likes Mary Anne!	$3.25
❑ MG43660-0	#11	Kristy and the Snobs	$3.25
❑ MG43721-6	#12	Claudia and the New Girl	$3.25
❑ MG43386-5	#13	Good-bye Stacey, Good-bye	$3.25
❑ MG43385-7	#14	Hello, Mallory	$3.25
❑ MG43717-8	#15	Little Miss Stoneybrook...and Dawn	$3.25
❑ MG44234-1	#16	Jessi's Secret Language	$3.25
❑ MG43659-7	#17	Mary Anne's Bad-Luck Mystery	$3.25
❑ MG43718-6	#18	Stacey's Mistake	$3.25
❑ MG43510-8	#19	Claudia and the Bad Joke	$3.25
❑ MG43722-4	#20	Kristy and the Walking Disaster	$3.25
❑ MG43507-8	#21	Mallory and the Trouble with Twins	$3.25
❑ MG43658-9	#22	Jessi Ramsey, Pet-sitter	$3.25
❑ MG43900-6	#23	Dawn on the Coast	$3.25
❑ MG43506-X	#24	Kristy and the Mother's Day Surprise	$3.25
❑ MG43347-4	#25	Mary Anne and the Search for Tigger	$3.25
❑ MG42503-X	#26	Claudia and the Sad Good-bye	$3.25
❑ MG42502-1	#27	Jessi and the Superbrat	$3.25
❑ MG42501-3	#28	Welcome Back, Stacey!	$3.25
❑ MG42500-5	#29	Mallory and the Mystery Diary	$3.25
❑ MG42498-X	#30	Mary Anne and the Great Romance	$3.25
❑ MG42497-1	#31	Dawn's Wicked Stepsister	$3.25
❑ MG42496-3	#32	Kristy and the Secret of Susan	$3.25
❑ MG42495-5	#33	Claudia and the Great Search	$3.25
❑ MG42494-7	#34	Mary Anne and Too Many Boys	$3.25
❑ MG42508-0	#35	Stacey and the Mystery of Stoneybrook	$3.25
❑ MG43565-5	#36	Jessi's Baby-sitter	$3.25
❑ MG43566-3	#37	Dawn and the Older Boy	$3.25
❑ MG43567-1	#38	Kristy's Mystery Admirer	$3.25

More titles... ▶

The Baby-sitters Club titles continued...

❑ MG43568-X	#39 Poor Mallory!	$3.25
❑ MG44082-9	#40 Claudia and the Middle School Mystery	$3.25
❑ MG43570-1	#41 Mary Anne Versus Logan	$3.25
❑ MG44083-7	#42 Jessi and the Dance School Phantom	$3.25
❑ MG43572-8	#43 Stacey's Emergency	$3.25
❑ MG43573-6	#44 Dawn and the Big Sleepover	$3.25
❑ MG43574-4	#45 Kristy and the Baby Parade	$3.25
❑ MG43569-8	#46 Mary Anne Misses Logan	$3.25
❑ MG44971-0	#47 Mallory on Strike	$3.25
❑ MG43571-X	#48 Jessi's Wish	$3.25
❑ MG44970-2	#49 Claudia and the Genius of Elm Street	$3.25
❑ MG44969-9	#50 Dawn's Big Date	$3.25
❑ MG44968-0	#51 Stacey's Ex-Best Friend	$3.25
❑ MG44966-4	#52 Mary Anne + 2 Many Babies	$3.25
❑ MG44967-2	#53 Kristy for President	$3.25
❑ MG44965-6	#54 Mallory and the Dream Horse	$3.25
❑ MG44964-8	#55 Jessi's Gold Medal	$3.25
❑ MG45657-1	#56 Keep Out, Claudia!	$3.25
❑ MG45658-X	#57 Dawn Saves the Planet	$3.25
❑ MG45659-8	#58 Stacey's Choice	$3.25
❑ MG45660-1	#59 Mallory Hates Boys (and Gym)	$3.25
❑ MG45662-8	#60 Mary Anne's Makeover	$3.50
❑ MG45663-6	#61 Jessi and the Awful Secret	$3.50
❑ MG45575-3	Logan's Story Special Edition Readers' Request	$3.25

Available wherever you buy books...or use this order form.

Scholastic Inc., P.O. Box 7502, 2931 E. McCarty Street, Jefferson City, MO 65102

Please send me the books I have checked above. I am enclosing $_____
(please add $2.00 to cover shipping and handling). Send check or money order - no
cash or C.O.D.s please.

Name _____

Address _____

City_____ State/Zip_____

Tell us your birth date! _____

It's a Super Special Month!

YOU CAN WIN A TRIP TO WALT DISNEY WORLD RESORT®!

Enter The Winter Super Special Giveaway for The Baby-sitters Club® and Baby-sitters Little Sister® fans!

Visit Walt Disney World Resort...and experience all the excitement of Peter Pan, Tinkerbell, and a whole cast of characters! We'll send the **Grand Prize Winner** of this Giveaway and his/her parent or guardian (age 21 or older) on an all-expense paid trip, for 5 days and 4 nights, to Walt Disney World Resort in Florida!

> **10 Second Prize Winners get** a Baby-sitters Club Record Album!
> **25 Third Prize Winners get** a Baby-sitters Club T-shirt!

Just fill in the coupon below or write the information on a 3" x 5" piece of paper and mail to: THE WINTER SUPER SPECIAL GIVEAWAY, P.O. Box 7500, Jefferson City, MO 65102. Return by March 31, 1993.

Rules: Entries must be postmarked by March 31, 1993. Winners will be picked at random and notified by mail. No purchase necessary. Valid only in the U.S. Void where prohibited. Taxes on prizes are the responsibility of the winners and their immediate families. Employees of Scholastic Inc.; its agencies, affiliates, subsidiaries; and their immediate families are not eligible. For a complete list of winners, send a self-addressed stamped envelope after March 31, 1993 to: The Winter Super Special Giveaway Winners List, at the address provided above.

The Winter Super Special Giveaway

Name_____ Age _____

Street _____

City_____ State/Zip _____

Where did you buy this book?

☐ Bookstore ☐ Drugstore Supermarket ☐ Library
☐ Book Club ☐ Book Fair ☐ Other_____ (specify)

BSC692